Praise for the Ni⟨

"Top 10 Romance of 2012."
– Booklist, *The Night Is Mine*

"Top 5 Romance of 2012."
–NPR, *I Own the Dawn*

"Suzanne Brockmann fans will love this."
–Booklist, *Wait Until Dark*

"Best 5 Romance of 2013."
–Barnes & Noble, *Take Over at Midnight*

"Nominee for Reviewer's Choice Award
for Best Romantic Suspense of 2014."
–RT Book Reviews, *Light Up the Night*

Praise for the Firehawks series:

"Buchman again pens an excellent read!"
-RT Book Reviews, *Full Blaze*

Firehawks

Wildfire on the Skagit

Firehawks

Wildfire
on the Skagit

by
M. L. Buchman

Discover more by this author at:
www.mlbuchman.com

Cover images:
Helicopter flying over fire
© William Moneymaker | Dreamstime.com
Athletic young man outdoor
© Mircea Bezergheanu | Dreamstime.com
AKP-SmokejumperS082-06052009-Beda ©
https://www.flickr.com/photos/fortwainwright/3621399178
Pulaski Wildland Fireaxe © Jerimy Colbert (back cover)

Buchman Bookworks

Other works by this author:

Chapter 1

Guard your reserves!" The spotter shouted after he'd clambered from the cockpit, over all of the smokejumpers, and finally reached the back door of the roaring DC-3 jump plane.

Krista Thorson slapped her hand over her reserve parachute to make sure it didn't accidentally deploy when he popped open the door. A glance down the line assured her that all twelve smokejumpers in the flight were awake and doing the same.

A DC-3's cabin wasn't that cramped, until you piled wildland firefighting gear secure behind heavy cargo nets down one side, and a dozen fully geared up smokejumpers prone like beached whales down the other. They'd been trying to finish their night's sleep after the dawn call-to-fire, but the wildfire was so close to base that a catnap was all any of them had gotten.

Krista and Akbar "the Great" Jepps, the lead smokie, were always first stick. It had taken Krista a decade to work up to the Number Two slot. When Tim and before him TJ had still been on the crew, she was rarely out of the plane in the first pass—two jumpers was a typical stick for each passage of the plane over a jump spot.

It was a good, comfortable slot. Despite her constant threats to drop a tree on him and take over, she really wasn't interested in Lead; Akbar was just too damned good and she couldn't imagine jumping with anyone else.

Being Number Two in the first stick also meant that she got to test the air first, find a way down through the roaring winds so chaotic near a fire. She loved the challenge.

Fifteen minutes out from the fire they'd safety-checked each others' gear, from heavy jumpsuit pants secured at the boots so no tree branch could slip by, to parachute harness, to helmet with wire-mesh face mask. They were as ready as they could be.

Terry, Mount Hood Aviation's spotter for *Jump M1,* popped the rear door and pulled it inward. There was a slap of wind, especially where she and Akbar sat crammed at the rear of the plane—just the sort of slap that could snag a reserve parachute, then suck it and the attached smokie out the door after straining her through the metal hull.

Through the open door the smell of high mountain air and hot engine exhaust swirled about the cabin. The DC-3's big radial engines were no longer buffered by the airplane's thin hull, but now delivered their full-throated roar right into the open jump door—sweet music of the first jump of the fire season.

"Did you remember to call her this time?" Krista leaned down and shouted at Akbar. He was powerfully muscled, and over half a foot shorter than Krista's six feet plus. He was India's answer to Tom Cruise, except he was younger, fitter, and from Seattle. But just as short, which she'd usually remind him about now, but he was looking all freaked out.

"Crap!" He yanked out his cell phone as Krista laughed. He never remembered to warn his wife he was about to jump a fire and might not be able to call for days.

"You'd be lost without me, dude!"

"I'd be more lost without her," he shouted back.

Amazing, but true.

Akbar the Great had always been a rocking firefighter—there was a reason he was the lead smokie with such an elite outfit. He'd also been the crassest of womanizers. Right until the moment he met Laura Jenson. She'd done something to him, and not just stopping his ever-growing circle of post-fire flings.

He wasn't any less aggressive against a burn, but he was—

Krista searched for the right word.

—steadier?

Whatever it was, Laura had definitely been a good influence on Akbar. And on top of making Akbar behave, she was also a wilderness guide and expert horsewoman which made her real easy to respect. The fact that she was a totally likeable person just meant Akbar was way luckier than he deserved.

If he was a little less freaking happy all the time, he might be more tolerable. Of course, he was getting it regular from a wonderful woman, so maybe he had reason to be so goofy happy that Krista wanted to smack him sometimes.

Often.

What the hell. She smacked his shoulder hard.

"What was that for?" he shouted as he huddled over his phone.

"Just 'cause."

There was no way for Akbar to call now, not over the roar of engine and hundred mile-an-hour wind ripping by the door, so he sent a quick text Krista could see over his shoulder.

Fire.

"C'mon, dude. You been married a year and you still don't know shit." After a year—hell, Laura was a smart woman—after the first twenty minutes, she must have known what sort of a man Akbar was. Didn't mean that Krista couldn't tease him about it anyway.

"What?"

"You gotta tell her you love her or something. Most girls want to hear stuff like that."

He nodded about six times as if trying to embed that in his memory, but she knew it wouldn't stick.

"Now!"

"Oh, right." He scrambled out a quick "Hugs" on his phone and looked pretty pleased with himself. Sad.

Then he glanced up at her, as he stuffed away his phone. "Not you, though. I forget that Mama Krista is not like other girls."

Krista shrugged. All that romantic, mushy stuff had never done much for her. Still, if she hadn't learned to ignore that specific phrase from hearing it so many times that she was immune to it—mostly—she'd consider sending Akbar down without his parachute.

Not like other girls. She was too goddamn tall, broad-shouldered enough that guys (at least the ones with a death wish) asked if she played front four on the football team, and she was stronger than any of them. *Not like other girls*, had plagued her since birth. If she—

Krista shoved her growing anger aside, pissed that it had slid up around her guard yet again.

"Dropping," Terry shouted from where he'd been leaning out the door and assessing the terrain and fire below. He'd been shouting instructions to the pilot over the headset.

Akbar turned off his phone and stuffed it into his personal gear bag along with his food and water. Then they both scooted up close beside the spotter.

Terry kept to the leading edge of the open door—he had a solid safety line snapped to his harness so that he was secure despite leaning halfway out the door. He also wore a parachute just in case, but not the full jump gear—if he ever had to bail out over a forest, his landing was gonna hurt.

He tossed a trio of crepe paper streamers. They were a dozen feet long, a foot wide, and weighted so that they'd fall at least a little like a smokie in a parachute.

Krista looked out at the evergreen forest and the fire. *Jump M1* flew just fifteen hundred feet over a classic Pacific Northwest vista. The Cascades were sharp mountains, heaving multiple rocky crags up past eight thousand feet. And today's fire placed the massive rounded peak of Mt. Rainier's fourteen-thousand feet in the foreground. The early morning sunlight glittering off the glacier-covered dormant volcano was almost painfully bright despite her sunglasses.

At the mountain's foot lay steep ridge-and-valley country covered in a solid carpet of dark summer green, near enough black with the shadows of the sun's low angle. Some maple and alder, but these slopes were mostly spruce and two-hundred foot Douglas fir just waiting to snag a smokie who didn't nail the drop zone.

The fire was a dozen acres and growing aggressively up three different valleys at once. The tail of the fire was down low in a creek-bed valley running between the two ridges which told Krista it was probably human caused. Lightning fires typically started up high and often in a dozen spots at once. Multiple points of origin low in the valley would point to arson. Single point of origin down in the valley meant it was a runaway campfire or some idiot hunter with exploding targets.

The black, red, and gold streamers—the MHA logo colors— fell cleanly for the first five hundred feet. Then they jinked hard to the south. One of the streamers spun off northwest. The other two practically tied themselves in a knot. Then for the last five hundred feet the pair of streamers shot back north, eventually disappearing into the trees almost exactly straight below where they'd been tossed out.

Terry looked up at them, "You saw?" he shouted.

They both nodded dutifully.

"I make it a hard ride with almost no drift overall. Your drop zone is that small clearing just south of the tail of the fire. Watch for catching the northerly drift current taking you right into the fire."

Krista leaned out to look back at the spot Terry had picked out. A hundred-foot wide hole in the middle of two hundred-foot trees. A real squeak when flying a thirty-foot wide ram chute.

"Race your ass to dead center," she yelled at Akbar. "First round of drinks at the Doghouse."

He held up a hand to accept the challenge and she high-fived it; she loved free beer. He might be married-weirdo-in-love, but he was a fantastic jump partner—even if she was more accurate than he was. The boy just never learned.

The plane circled back and started the climb to jump altitude at three thousand feet above the ground—fifteen hundred feet of free fall in the first five seconds and sixty seconds of madness after the chute deployed. It was the best ride a girl could find. She and Akbar did final four-point checks on their own parachute controls: harness secure, release ripcord across chest, cutaway for the main chute if there was a problem, reserve release at hand.

"In the door," Terry yelled.

Krista glanced one last time at the other smokies. They were all plastered up against the small round windows to see what they could of the fire and streamers. In their bulky jumpsuits and heavy gear, they were awkward and looked utterly ridiculous everywhere except jumping on a fire.

Most of the crew were seasoned MHA regulars that she'd spent a half dozen seasons jumping with. But there were also one rookie and two snookies—second year rookies—she'd be keeping an eye on. MHA never had a true rookie, because the Forest Circus—as the U.S. Forest Service was universally called among smokies—or Bureau of Land Management trained them for a year or two first. But even five-year jump veterans like the newest hire, Evan Greene, were dubbed "rookies" when they joined MHA.

She'd made a point of running practice jumps with every new recruit to Mount Hood Aviation's smokejumper team and hadn't seen a thing to complain about. The snookies in this load were good, two years each jumping with the BLM before shifting to her outfit.

But Rookie Evan Greene from the Montana Zulies was a cut above. That had been clear from the moment he'd stepped into the parachute loft at MHA's small jump base high in the foothills of Oregon's Mount Hood—eleven thousand feet of dormant volcano loomed over their camp.

That day the loft had contained a milling hoard of returning jumpers, packing chutes after their pre-season re-certification jumps. They'd been playing grab-ass and catching up on who had done what with whom off season. Riverboat had made a couple season's worth of pay at the poker table, and Crash had spent the winter skiing and teaching classes for eligible snow bunnies up at Sun Valley. Most had jumped bushfires in Australia with Krista last year and had only a month off, but still she made them re-certify to be on the MHA roster.

And even in that high-jump crowd, Evan Greene had stood out like a sore thumb, well, a not-sore thumb. Damn but the bastard was dark-eyed and handsome even if he didn't lord it about. He was pure business during the interview, the check ride and jump, and all of the last three weeks of pre-season conditioning.

He never ran at the front of the pack on the daily grinds, though it was clear he easily could have. Instead, he hung next to someone having trouble and cheered them along until they did more than they thought they could. Exactly the kind of guy MHA was always looking for.

Even now, sitting at the end of the lineup on the plane, Evan stood out. He had the big, powerful build most smokies developed, but he also exuded a confidence that was hard to look away from. No way was Krista going to get involved with any rookie, but if she was, he'd definitely look like Evan Greene. Krista returned her attention to her upcoming jump, at least most of it. She could feel the rookie watching her. Only natural, everyone always watched the first stick jumpers all the way down to see what their own ride was going to be like.

Akbar shifted from kneeling just inside the door beside Terry until he sat in the doorway, his feet out in the wind and dangling over empty space.

Krista moved in to stand close behind him. MHA Smokies jumped in pairs, one from sitting and one from standing. On some planes sticks could be three or four in a row rushing out the door, but the old DC-3 simply didn't lend itself to that between the low door and the tail section not far past the door.

Just like always she nudged her boots against Akbar's butt as if she was going to kick him out early. He kept his hands braced on the inside edge of the doorway, but he barked out, "Don't even!" as he did every time. Part of their jump ritual, it brought good luck.

Terry stuck his head around the corner of the doorway and looked out past Akbar. He yelled something to the pilot over the headset and the DC-3 sideslipped to a new alignment on the drop zone.

"Standby."

Akbar shifted his grip low in the door, now ready to yank himself out the door rather than making sure he stayed in. She did the same higher up on the doorframe.

Terry raised his hand and Krista focused on that alone.

Terry slapped Akbar's shoulder and he yanked himself out the door. Krista was moving before Akbar's weight was even off the toes of her boots. She yanked herself out and down to clear the tail section.

In moments, she was flying.

# # #

Evan Greene leaned up against the DC-3's window and watched as Akbar and Krista tumbled down to earth. Under his breath he counted with them:

"Jump-thousand. Look-thousand," he could see them spinning about to scan in all directions. "Reach-thousand," too far away now to see their hands on their ripcords. "Wait-thousand." "Pull-thousand," and their chutes bloomed in unison, big rectangular ram chutes in black, red, and gold. Krista floated well above Akbar.

When the plane circled in the opposite direction, he lost sight of them. The seasoned MHA smokies must have known their pilot's habits because they were on the move before Evan sensed the beginning of the turn. They all shifted to the other side of the plane to keep an eye on the jumpers. Which left him a crappy view over Ox's shoulder. Couldn't see much at all.

"Wild, rookie," Gustav the Ox teased him. "Don't know if you can handle this one. Maybe you should stay aboard rather than risking that purdy face of yours in them big, bad trees."

"Willing to put money on that?" Evan's rookie year had been five years ago with the Zulies out of Missoula, Montana, one of the hottest smoke teams in the Forest Service. He'd been in solid for every summer, but the winters off the fire were hard. He didn't like the downtime—always spent the winters looking for something to do with his time. He didn't do "stop" worth crap.

MHA had promised more, they jumped off-season to the southern hemisphere fires. "Sold out" some of the Zulies had accused him, for his leaving the USFS and joining a civilian outfit. Often the same ones who'd teased him in public had pulled him aside in private and made him promise to report back.

"Hell, boy," Ox drawled out in his best country-hick accent. "Your gear don't even smell of wood smoke."

Protesting about the fact that MHA had issued him brand new gear would have no effect whatsoever, so he didn't bother.

"Besides," Ox sneered at him, "You're a rookie. We've got a rule against taking rookie money…except at poker."

"Don't play," Evan did, but not well enough to take on a table of smokejumpers. "You play pool and you're on."

"Done!" Ox agreed as the line shuffled forward.

Evan had bought his first car by pool sharking in Boise. He'd show Ox a thing or two for calling him rookie. Even if it was pretty standard hazing for the "new guy," after five years jumping fire, it got under his skin a bit.

They were sixth and last stick, placing Evan at the very tail of the line. He tried not to take it personally, but he did. He'd always been in the first few sticks with the Zulies, often jumping lead on secondary fires. Was it because he was once again a rookie after five years of jumping that he was at the back or was it really just the chance of the rotation after the first stick, as the MHA jumpers insisted?

As the plane circled around to drop the next stick, Evan delayed long enough to get a good look out the window at Akbar and Krista circling down into the hole in the trees. Akbar made it down, stalling his chute hard and doing a roll between two trees at the edge of the small clearing. Clean jump.

Krista had done his initial interview and been his test-jump partner when he'd come down to Mount Hood Aviation's base camp just south of Hood River, Oregon.

He'd remembered the feeling as she yanked on his gear during the buddy check, making sure everything was in place and properly attached. She'd given tips that he hadn't learned in five years of jumping with the Zulies—little things, so small they barely mattered—which told him more about MHA than anything else had. Even the tiniest bit safer mattered deeply to these people.

Evan had been terribly self-conscious as he'd checked Krista's gear. Female smokejumpers were rare, it was just too hard physically. IHCs, sure. More and more women were fighting fire from the ground crews. Tough hikes, long days, and hard work, it's what the Interagency Hotshot Crews were good at and some of the women did great.

Smokies didn't fight fire, they battled it. It was the Special Forces posting of the civilian world. That's why he gravitated to jumping fire after six years in the Green Berets—a past he did not advertise. And before that there was the past he did his best to forget. Better everyone though he'd been hatched out as a smokejumper from the first day.

When women did make the jump lineup—and the Zulies had a couple—they were about as sexy as battering rams. All grit and determination and in your face about it. Like they were trying to be more macho than the guys and always being aware that they were the outsider long after the guys had forgotten about it.

The next two sticks jumped and the ride down was a wild one, but he watched them to the ground trying to map the shifting of the unseen winds in his head to plan his own route down.

Krista Thorson was something else, first stick of jumpers at an outfit like MHA said that it wasn't honorary either. There were women trying to make Special Forces, but they just didn't have the upper body strength to qualify no matter how driven they were.

Krista would have had no problems there. She was built on a grand scale. Tall enough to look him square in the eye, broad of frame, big chested, and sassy as hell. Her powerful shoulders emphasized by the brush of light-blond hair—a smooth fall that set off a great face and the bluest eyes he'd ever seen.

She had a fast wit, a mouth that was always on the verge of a laugh, and she moved like a Master Sergeant—with the casual power of someone who knew that the battle wouldn't even begin without her there. Master Sergeants were called the backbone of the military for a reason and Krista was clearly the Number Two smokie for the same one.

He checked his gear for about the tenth time. He was always a little extra paranoid, but it served him well as a Special Forces Green Beret and so far it had served him well as a smokie.

Krista was not his usual type; not at all. He typically went for the long and slender ones who populated the smokejumper bars and the Special Forces bars before that.

But he'd practically blushed when checking Krista's parachute harness just above those big breasts visible even through the jumpsuit. He couldn't help wondering what it would be like to wrestle with that much woman, both her confidence and her body.

And his body's reaction to those thoughts inside full jump gear was decidedly uncomfortable—the material too thick and the jump harness too tight to let him rearrange anything from the outside.

The next to last stick jumped. He took one last look out the window before scooting up behind Ox.

Krista had floated down to land dead center in the deep hole among the trees. Tuck and roll, then she popped back to her feet and was standing on Akbar's collapsed chute as if counting coup.

Damn but she could fly.

# # #

Krista stood at the edge of the jump spot and watched them coming in. It was the sort of place to have a picnic, green, unspoiled, and it would be sunny and warm once the sun was high enough.

It was hard to believe that two hundred feet north through thick trees and thicker undergrowth, a fire raged leaving behind only scorched earth and blackened stumps.

When Tim Harada had left to take over the lead slot for the Alaska Fire Service—after falling in love with his Alaska hometown sweetheart, real damn sad—Akbar had tagged Krista as his Number Two. Which in her mind meant that it was now up to her to uphold the advantages of singlehood for the rest of the crew.

The lead men were such total saps, both Tim and Akbar falling in love like that. She wouldn't have bet on it lasting a season for either of them—hell, she wouldn't have bet it was even possible…not until she'd met the women. They made it easy to imagine the marriages lasting a lifetime. Just too weird.

Not in her future; not while she was jumping. Probably not after, but that thought didn't bother her as much as it used to.

The only smokies who remained stable in relationships were single or dead—marriage for wildland firefighters was nuts, plain and simple. Smokies spent all summer and fall gone to fire; and lately—with MHA's taste for southern hemisphere contracts—winters as well.

In addition to upholding bachelorette-hood, it also fell to her to make sure everyone was up to snuff and safe. She now assessed each one of them coming in as she jammed her chute into a stuff sack. First jump of the season was always especially worrisome.

The DC-3, painted gloss black with red-and-orange flames tracing down its length, made multiple passes, dropping only one stick at a time. The winds were too chaotic for two sticks to jump and all have a good chance of hitting the drop zone.

She could see that Axe and the Jackal—last name Jackson and could howl like a coyote—were jumping clean.

Ant-man caught a bad downdraft and plummeted the moment he crossed the edge of the clearing.

Krista held her breath.

His real name was Lee, but on his second-ever fire he'd slept next to an anthill and been forced to constantly beat them out of his food bag for the rest of the fire. At least he wasn't Fire-ant-man.

A little hard maneuvering and he managed to save it, slamming through the treetops and snagging his chute about a hundred feet up. His curses were plenty audible down on the ground as he dug his let-down rope out of the thigh-pocket of his jumpsuit. Ant-man's curses grew even louder when his jump partner, Nick the Greek—who was neither named Nick nor was he Greek, but had made an injudicious remark a couple years back about wanting to nail Nikki and her big breasts in My Big Fat Greek Wedding—hit his landing dead on the mark.

Others came in more or less clean, two treed in the towering branches of an unburned Doug fir, but no injuries. Eight down and packing their jump gear, two in the trees and moving carefully to make sure they didn't knock themselves loose and plummet to the ground.

Last stick, Ox came in as clean as a seasoned pro. He was built on Krista's scale, big and powerful. He had this weird taste for pixie-sized women about as big around as his bicep. It was a wonder he didn't break them; they always looked so frail beside him. Hell of a smokie though.

Krista preferred her lovers to have enough substance for a good tussle. She never dated inside the squad, just wouldn't do. And finding extra-curricular men up to smokie standards made for sparse pickings, but she didn't do badly despite not suffering from the modern American image of beauty. Not like high school which had totally sucked.

Ox's rookie jump-partner caught the reverse of the bad gust that had treed Ant-man. Instead of losing most of the lift as he approached the drop zone, he was whisked back aloft on a hot thermal.

Evan Greene was there one moment and simply gone the next. Gone straight toward the fire and not a thing that even the best jumper could do about it.

Shit!

"Ox! Jackal!" She grabbed a Pulaski fire axe and bolted into the trees.

# # #

Evan had tried a hard turn while stalling the chute to get clear of the thermal, but it hadn't let him down in time. He was jerked back aloft and the drop zone was now gone behind him—no way to get it back.

Need alternate landing. You got about ten seconds, Ev.

Down here near the valley floor, the trees were massive. Snagging a tree two hundred feet up was incredibly dangerous. He'd be as likely to collapse the chute and plummet down as to get safely stuck and then lower himself to the ground.

The only places not thick with trees were…mostly on fire.

The tail of the fire didn't have the towering flames like the ones he'd seen up at the head, but it was still burning outward in all directions despite the lack of driving wind.

He relaxed the steering toggles to get maximum flight distance. The burning edge of the fire gave him some welcome extra lift, but not enough to turn back. Even though the slap of heat punched right through his gear and the smoke stung his eyes, it bought him a hundred feet up and another few seconds of descent.

Past the burning edge, he entered the Black—the burned-out forest that was stark with loss of color. Greens and browns had been stripped away, replaced by black char, tree bark scorched gray, and all wrapped in writhing smoke that made it look like a horror movie set.

The trees still stood, might even still be alive. But without the cushioning smaller branches and foliage—which had all been burned away—the main branches were as brittle and dangerous as blackened spears.

Despite the wind of his passage, there was a silence above the Black. He could hear the trickling of a stream rolling fast over rounded rocks, a glistening silver line in the gray world. The low fires of the tail now crackled a hundred meters behind him.

A landing spot.

Well, not even a spot, more of a narrow slot. A small ridge of rock had kept the big trees clear to either side. The fire had cleared it of brush and saplings.

He was running with the wind. He flew past his new drop zone and did his best not to look at the fast approaching spires of taller trunks on the climbing slope.

Evan yanked down on the parachute's left steering toggle, initiating a braked flat turn and spun like a top right around the nastiest looking of the still standing trees. Then he dove into the headwind.

As soon as he cleared the leading edge of the opening over the narrow bit of rock, he stalled the parachute hard. The ground rushed up toward him. At the last moment he flared the chute converting most of his speed into lift, and managed to land with just enough impact that he had to do a tuck and roll but was able to regain his feet. A quick twist and he collapsed the chute before it snagged any of the trees.

A voice spoke from close behind him, making him jump.

"You better not have gotten any burn holes in that chute, Rookie, or Chutes will take it out of your hide." Chutes was the master of MHA's parachute loft and hell on anyone who packed a chute that was less than perfect.

Evan spun to see Krista standing just two steps away. She must have sprinted the whole way upslope from the drop zone to get here so fast. Winded, though not badly, she wore her hardhat and gripped a well-worn Pulaski in her gloved hands.

"Just thought I'd do a little sightseeing before I started on the fire," and he turned back to gathering his chute. Soon his heart rate would start coming down. It was always crazy on landing, even on a clean one. Missing the drop zone and nearly eating a smokie-killing tree had pumped his pulse up with a serious dose of adrenaline along the way.

Krista standing so close and grinning at him wasn't helping.

"Good jump, Rook. That was a really nice save. Could get to like you. Just don't go off worrying me again without permission."

"Yes, sir," he saluted sharply.

"Do I look like a *sir?*" She cupped her big hands beneath her breasts which were framed by the chest and waist straps of her safety harness. "These aren't over-muscled pecs, Rook."

"Wouldn't know, sir," he nodded toward her chest. "You haven't shown them to me."

She saluted back, but he could tell it was a civilian gesture; and not just because it was made with a middle finger flicked against the brim of her hardhat and a laugh.

Still, Master Sergeant Krista Thorson definitely fit her— military or not. Odd, he knew the background of most of the crew after the three weeks of season-prep and dozens of practice jumps.

He knew nothing about Krista.

Chapter 2

*T*heir *cargo dropped in* clean and they soon had the drop zone secure. Akbar led half of the team up the right flank of the fire, leaving her to lead the rest of them to the left.

"Nick the Greek," Krista pointed downslope. "I want you to get a pump anchored down at the stream. Once Ant-man gets back out of his tree, run a couple hoses. I want you to focus on killing the tail."

"You hear that?" Nick shouted up at the tree.

Ant-man had lowered himself down safely, and was now climbing back up into the tree to retrieve his chute. "Is that shit speaking?" a shout sounded from seventy or eighty feet up in the thick branches.

Nick turned back to Krista, "We got ya covered." His evil grin said that Ant-man was a long way from living down his tree landing.

But if Nick said they had the situation under control, there was no doubt they did.

"Axe, Jackal, Ox, and Rookie," she turned to the remaining smokies, "you're with me."

"I have a name," Evan protested. "It's—"

"Not yet you don't," Ox's deep voice shut him down. "You don't got a name until Mama Krista tags you. Until then, you're just Rook."

Krista offered Evan a smirk to keep him in his place. She might have cut him some slack if he hadn't scared her by flying into the Black. The Black was more dangerous than tall trees, but he'd flown a perfect pattern. She doubted if she could have done better; man was a born jumper.

"Give me a goddamn break, Ox," he groaned but you could tell he knew it wouldn't do any good and was just fighting the good fight.

"Nope!" As they bantered, Evan was sorting through the piled up gear just like the rest of them.

The parachutes and reserves were all stuffed into a big sack to be sorted out and repacked back at base. They rummaged through the fatboy boxes for food. Snickers went fast and vegetarian MRE's went slow—because veggie-anything Meals, Ready-to-Eat weren't fit to be eaten. Not by woman or beast.

They also loaded up on Pulaski fire-axes, chainsaws, and a jerry can of gasoline. They all drank their water bottles dry, refilled them, and Ox added the rest of the five-gallon cube of water to his load—they'd drain it fast enough.

Akbar and four smokies had gone to the right flank, Krista led her four up the left, leaving Nick and Ant-man to deal with the tail.

The fire wasn't very active up the left flank. They beat it back with cut-off pine boughs and shovelfuls of dirt. The smaller trees that were burning, they cut and dropped them back into the fire. When a bigger one was burning, they'd cut away the small trees around it that were not yet burned so that the bigger tree couldn't spark across. Ones that were really bad—snags getting ready to fall across the line or clearly dead and looking for a smokie to drop on—they cut and dropped back into the fire and attacked it with more dirt.

With a little quick handwork as they climbed, they ensured that the lower flanks of the fire weren't spreading any further before the hose team could get to them. A big wind shift might drive the flames, but there wasn't one predicted this morning. And by the time the afternoon heat hit, this flank should be burned down, soaked with stream water by Nick and Antman, and not up to threatening anyone.

The team moved with all the kinks of the first fire of the season. Knee problems, wrenched lower backs, and old shoulder injuries wouldn't start surfacing until later in the season, but they all moved like a bunch of rookies. Digging a line with the hoe side of his Pulaski, Jackal almost nutted Axe with his handle. Ox was so head-down on the line he was digging that he actually walked sideways right into a burning tree. The only one working clean at the moment was the rookie.

"Hey," she couldn't resist. "Is the Rook the only one who remembers how to fight a fire?"

The crew grumbled but started falling into a cleaner rhythm. Pity about the rookie not giving her anything to tease him about.

Five hundred feet vertical and a half-mile up the slope, she called a brief halt. Two hours had passed with hardly a pause. The next three thousand feet up would not go nearly as quickly.

"Take ten," she called.

Several of the smokies simply dropped to the ground. At this point it wasn't exhaustion, but rather energy conservation. Sitting on the ground and letting your muscles relax for ten minutes would pay off tenfold if they had to be on the fire for a couple of days straight.

Evan kicked a log out of the fire and dug a steel mug out of his personal gear bag. He filled it with water from the half-empty water cube and set the mug right on the coals of the wood. Standard smokie practice would have him dumping two or three instant coffee packets into the cup, probably swallowing one dry on top of it.

"Should save the caffeine for later, Rook," Krista scowled down at him. "Or are you so out of shape that you need it already?"

He grinned up at her and dug into his PG bag. He didn't pull out an instant coffee packet. Instead, he pulled out a pouch of hot chocolate and flapped it at her before dumping it into his rapidly heating cup.

Krista did what she could to suppress her laugh, "With or without the marshmallows?"

"With, of course. Only way to drink it."

"Rookies," she did her best to sound disgusted as she shook her head sadly.

"Hey, I've got skills," he grinned up at her as he stirred his cocoa in with a stick and then pulled on a glove so that he could lift the mug off the burning log. He kicked the log back into the flames and sipped contentedly, making loud "Ahh!" noises.

"Remind me if I ever need a cocoa expert on the fireline."

"Honor to serve, Master Sergeant."

Krista could see the urge to salute still rooted deep in the man. She'd met enough of them in her time to recognize a soldier turned firefighter. Most did well, except for the poor suckers who weren't ready when the fire triggered PTSD. Maybe he hadn't served front lines, or maybe he'd gotten it out of his system during his years with the Zulies. She'd have to wait and see.

Until Krista was more sure of him, she wasn't going to risk letting him too far out of her sight.

She turned away to survey the fire.

It was making noises, but not the deep-throated wildfire roar that would deafen them higher up the valley. She heard shouting voices sounding up faintly from below.

"Rook," she called without turning.

"Yo!"

"When you're done with your after-school snack, trot down the slope and find out how Ant-man and Nick the Greek are doing on the tail."

"Radio broken, Master Sergeant?" he joshed her, but slugged back his cocoa and was disappearing down the slope before she could respond.

No, her radio worked just fine. Smokies hated going downslope when they'd just have to come back. So, test one: did he respond well to orders? Now answered with a yes. Test two: how clear would his communication and observations be as he went down and back up the line?

Third, it was always a good practice to send a man back over a finished line every now and then to make sure no sparks had jumped over. Especially when the firebreak was as narrow as the one they'd cut around the tail.

Four? There was a fourth reason there, but she wasn't so sure what it was.

Just before he disappeared over a small rise and down into the smoke, he turned back and saluted. She could see from his smile that he knew exactly what she was doing...even if she didn't.

Which pissed her off all the more.

"Okay. Enough lazing about," she told the other smokies. "Let's hurt a little." It came out harsher than she intended.

But the others were on their feet in seconds and they prepared to attack the fire's flank up the face of the ridge with no more than the usual complaints. This next section was going to be tougher and much hotter. In five minutes they'd forget they'd had a break at all, in ten their bodies would start wondering when the next one would be.

She could hear the helos working the head of the fire and Akbar calling on the command frequency. His people were at the same elevation as her team but on the far side of the fire, working upslope, making sure it didn't spread sideways. She could picture Akbar right there across the Black. Less than a half mile away, invisible beyond the smoke-wreathed land that lacked even the least speck of green.

Mr. Lovesick…no. Mr. Lovedrunk…not that either. Akbar was…just too damned happy. He'd always been an upbeat guy, but watching him with Laura was enough to make a girl's teeth ache because they were so damn sweet together.

Krista turned away to assess the slope and the fire ahead.

It was time to leave the Black behind and start cutting a serious fireline. From now until they met Akbar's team around the head of the fire, the teams would be separated by fire, not by char. They'd trade nose-tickling carbon for the sweetness of burning sap.

If there was a flareup, her people still had a good escape to the west, but it wouldn't be any fun. Their best escape would be to create a wide fireline that the flames couldn't breach—which was the whole point anyway.

"Give me a break ten yards wide," she called out, having to raise her voice to be heard over the fire. It was all the direction they needed. Akbar had taken the two snookies, so these four were all hard-seasoned MHA firefighters.

Axe and Jackal fired off their chainsaws, Ox began clearing what they'd cut to the far side of the firebreak. Not many guys could swamp for two sawyers at the same time, but Ox could. He dragged branches and rolled sections of tree trunk through thick brush to get it well clear of the fire's edge. Ten yards of fireline cleared of flammable fuels. Another five hundred feet up, they'd have to double the width of the line.

Krista came along behind the team and worked the soil with her Pulaski, cutting a line down through all of the organics. She dragged the highly flammable top layers of dried leaves and needles back a dozen feet so that they didn't catch any embers. The underground organics she cleared from a yard-wide swath. Even a small gap of exposed mineral soils could stop a ground fire that was creeping through the duff.

Krista wasn't much of a one for deep thinking, but she did wonder why she'd decided she should keep a close eye on the rookie and then sent him downslope just moments later. The first decision was a safety issue—Evan Greene was still an untested quantity. Sending him down the line was something else.

Instead of thinking about her team moving close above her or Akbar's team on the other flank or what the goddamn fire might be planning next, her thoughts were with a tall handsome rookie who kept saluting her like it meant something.

Not good.

She firmly turned her attention to the soil.

#

Evan cruised down the slope. At first he was glad of the chance to stretch out his legs after the first two hours of bent-over work.

He stopped only twice to shovel more soil over small flareups. The line was holding clean. He'd have made it wider, but Krista had called it dead on. She'd read the tail of the fire at some level he couldn't see, understood what it could and couldn't do with a master tactician's expertise.

Nick the Greek and Ant-man were working a pair of one-and-a-half inch hose lines along the tail. They had it doused hard and were now working up both sides at once.

"You guys going back to hotshotting?" Normally an Interagency Hotshot Crew would be here by now to do the lower-end handwork.

"Mount Hood Aviation is a full service firefighting outfit," Nick announced. Then grumbled, "Hell of a way to spend your first fire of the season. The access road washed out last winter. It was patched, but not well enough for any service vehicles, so the IHCs are hiking in. Still a couple hours out."

"I think Krista hates us," Ant-man had shut off his hose and come over when he saw Evan arrive.

"No, man," Nick sounded gleeful at the fresh opening. "She hates *you* for flying into a tree and *I'm* stuck suffering along with your sorry ass."

"Then she must hate me even worse," Evan drew some of the fire to spare Ant-man who was getting irritable, "for landing in the fire."

"How you figure that?"

"I've been sent down to check on you guys."

Ant-man looked at him strangely, "Her radio broken?"

"Nope," Evan did his best to sound cheerful, but he felt a little like a Private First Class who'd just been bucked back down to Private.

"Well, you gotta get her back, Man," Nick insisted. "Or you ain't no man."

Twenty minutes and a five hundred foot vertical climb later, Evan was wondering just who had been gotten back in this deal. Both of his arms were screaming: one from carrying five gallons of water, the other from hauling another five-gallon jerry can of chainsaw fuel. He'd stopped to switch off pretty often, not that it made any difference; they were both over forty pounds of goddamn heavy.

The guys had painted a picture of him striding back onto the line with the extra supplies and being welcomed like a returning hero. Instead he felt like a returning wet rag. The sun had cracked into the valley and on the occasions when it found a hole through the smoke, it cooked him in his gear. Nomex didn't burn easily, it also didn't breathe for shit. Give him some desert camos, a forty-pound ruck, and a combat rifle any day.

Well, at least a fire didn't shoot back much, but still.

Evan dug in and tried to find an easy-going stride as he crested the last rise into where they'd stopped for a break.

Effort wasted.

No one there.

He'd been gone thirty, maybe forty minutes, and the fire team was nowhere in sight. It might have been an elaborate dodge-the-rookie trick if it weren't for the fresh-cut fireline ranging up the slope ahead of him.

A slice had been made alongside the fire, a wide slice. To one side unburned forest so thick he couldn't see twenty feet in. To the other, flames were kicking up fifty, even a hundred feet into the sky. Even as he watched, smoke and ash from the active flank of the fire curled into the newly opened firebreak… and died.

A black-and-fire painted Firehawk helo roared down into the valley. Pounding in a hundred feet above the thick, unburned forest, it unleashed a long shower of a thousand gallons of bright red retardant to further guarantee that the fire didn't jump the new line. Little droplets of the retardant drifted over to land on him, tiny stings like bug bites everywhere it touched skin. Well, between the morning on the fire and the drop at least his gear wasn't stand-out pristine any more.

Once the helo peeled off, he could hear chainsaws chewing away at the trees above him, but they were out of sight in the smoke.

Had another team jumped in while he was gone to get so much done?

But as he trudged up the line, the crew slowly resolved into view. There were just four of them. Two sawyers, one swamper, and one who appeared to be everywhere at once.

Clearly in her natural element, Krista moved about the fireline like a blond ballerina in a hardhat. One moment she was digging line, the next she was helping Ox catch up with the sawyers. She ran a gas can up the line when one of the saws sputtered to a stop and they had it running again before Evan had closed half the distance.

Krista spotted him.

"Took your time, Rook."

"Brought you a present," Evan made a show of lifting the jerry can and the water cube though his arms wept when he did.

"Whoo-ee!" She hooted out. "Better than a bouquet of roses. We just might keep you, Rook." She hustled down the last of the slope and grabbed the jerry can.

He was about to protest about the weight, when she turned and trotted back up to the sawyers with it as if it was as light as that rose bouquet.

Roses for Krista? Evan was pretty sure he'd never given a woman other than Mom a bouquet of roses—and that had been for Mother's Day at a girlfriend's prompting. It wasn't until the girlfriend was long gone that he understood he should have given her flowers once in a while too. He just never thought of it. And his mother didn't deserve them. Neither of his parents had—ever.

By the time he reached the other near-empty water cube to set down his full one, Krista was back beside him.

"Take five, Rook. You earned it."

He wanted nothing more than to throw himself on the ground. Instead, he dug out a packet of electrolyte and dumped it into a dry water bottle. It was a challenge as his hands started shaking with the burn of lactic acid buildup in the muscles.

Krista watched him for a moment as he filled it from the cube.

"Nah," he did his best to make it sound casual. He slugged back half the bottle, knowing that would help more than any rest.

Clearly none of them had rested even a second of the time he'd been gone. It was the only way they could have gotten so much done. So resting wasn't an option, but he bought himself a few moments for the shakes to stop by giving his report. It also let him keep Krista to himself for a few moments. That was a feeling he definitely liked.

"The line below is clean. Only two small flare-ups and I buried them. Nick and Lee are moving well, though they need more hose dropped within the hour or they'll be down to a single line."

She hopped on the radio with that and one of the helos promised to make a drop.

He was as rested now as he was going to be on this fire. "Think I'll give Ox a hand." He took a step to go around Krista and she rested a hand on his shoulder.

She squeezed it hard, hard enough to rub bones together if he hadn't been muscled up for a fire season. "Thanks, Evan. You done good," her voice was surprisingly soft and smooth.

He flipped her a finger and grin just as she had done to him right after his jump into the Black.

As Evan moved up the slope he felt lighter than any other time during his entire first day with MHA.

It shouldn't matter that much that Krista had complimented him and used his real name. But it did.

And that smooth and silky tone in her voice…who knew a smokejumper could sound so sexy.

Chapter 3

The next time Evan was conscious of anything other than the fire, the sun was setting—for the second time.

The first afternoon's wind had brought flare-ups. Pitched battle had been engaged to keep the line. They were in country too steep for dozers and all the arrival of the Hotshot team had done was take over the flanks to free up MHA for the battle of the ridge.

One moment he'd be digging line, the next across the ridge and down in the unburned valley to the north with Ox killing off a spot fire.

As the wind kicked harder, they'd spent more and more of their time scrambling up and down the treacherous terrain killing nascent fires that embers were trying to spark on the next slope.

In the quiet of the night they'd desperately cut more line trying to save the next valley over and then spent the entire second day defending that line.

It was the evening of Day Two when he ground to a halt.

The smokies all finished together high up in the saddle between two peaks. They just stood in the high clearing and looked dazedly about. Evan knew he was no better off than those around him, blinking hard in surprise at the sudden lack of anything to do.

In front of them, the fire snapped and spat.

But they'd contained it and it wasn't going anywhere.

The MHA helicopters were already down for the night—Forest Service contract said they were out of the sky from a half hour before sunset to a half hour after sunrise. Sometimes night operations were authorized, along with the stiff extra fee, but it wasn't needed on this fire. All the fire needed tonight was a lookout, making sure it didn't escape as it finished burning the woods inside the fireline.

Behind them was a hundred thousand acres of untouched forest lands except for a few charred spots where they'd beaten down spot fires—not one of them bigger than an acre.

"Camping here," Akbar croaked in a voice hoarse with firesmoke and exhaustion.

Still there was little movement. Nick the Greek may have been the first one to drop to one knee, but in the next second everyone was down on the ground except Krista.

Evan watched as she started gathering kindling and firewood.

He forced his own legs—rubbery from two days and a night on the line—into motion and clambered down across the fireline to fetch a brand from the sputtering fire. He chose a well-burned branch still flaming hot enough at one end to start a campfire easily.

He made it back up the hill—barely—and rammed it into Krista's pile of wood before sitting down. He wound up next to Krista.

She'd shed her hardhat, jacket, and long-sleeved fire shirt. All she wore now was a sweat-stained cotton t-shirt that clung to every curve and outline. Stretched wide across her breasts the shirt declared, "Smokejumpers do it best in a fire."

He was staring. He knew it, but damn.

# # #

"Good first fire, Rook," Krista could see Evan battling to look her in the face rather than the chest. It was kind of sweet actually. Most men either talked directly to her breasts or took one gander at her solid frame and went looking somewhere else.

She'd been built to be on the football team, not the cheerleading squad. Not that the high school in Concrete, Washington had much of either one, but they tried. She'd been told to go out for shot put and she'd told them to go to hell.

And here was this guy, looking her in the eyes now, like she was something special. Absolutely no one had ever done that. Not even her father, though he was so meek he never looked anyone in the eye, and spoke only rarely. It was likely she'd inherited all the brass Pop had never found.

"First fire. Yeah," Evan's voice sounded as tired as she felt. "The Zulies never let me actually fight a fire before. I was just a water boy for them."

"That's what they told us, too." Krista knew he'd been top five over there. Top five jumper with the Zulies meant MHA was damned lucky to get him.

She pulled her big knife out of its thigh sheath, a well-worn, Vietnam-era K-bar. She sliced open a pair of MREs with the ease of long practice and slipped it back into the sheath.

"There's a *Don't Mess With Me* message if ever I saw one," Evan pulled out a much newer but equally worn K-bar Becker and did the same to a couple of MREs of his own.

"Grandpop's," she explained tapping her sheath.

"Mine," he resheathed his blade.

She could see it in him. It wasn't posturing or bragging; it was just part of who he was. She'd barely glanced at his resume because she didn't trust such things, preferred her own judgments about people. But she recalled some stretch of U.S. Army time before he'd gone to smokejumping.

One of his meals was the Mexican Style Chicken Stew. He pulled out another packet of that hot chocolate and sprinkled it into the pouch.

"What the hell, Rook?"

"Mole sauce," he finished sprinkling. He picked out the dehydrated marshmallows and, popping them into his mouth, began sucking on them like candy.

"Got some extra?" She'd drawn a Chili with Beans which was okay, but she liked the idea of Mexican.

He handed her the half empty packet which she dumped in.

They each set their foil packets on a rock around the campfire and sat back to wait for the meals to heat from totally disgusting—the way they were normally eaten on a fire—to warmly awful.

The others were doing the same. Ox had four fat frankfurters that he was cooking on an alder branch.

"Hey," Nick the Greek called out. "Where the hell you get those?"

"Stuffed 'em into my PG bag hard frozen before we jumped. They're thawed now."

"Two days, dude. In your Personal Gear? More like ripe!"

"Just the way I like 'em."

"Got any ants this time?" Nick called to Lee, looking for the next target.

"Not a one," Ant-man said proudly. "Might have slipped a small snake into your bag though."

Krista let the banter run back and forth across the fire without joining in. Normally she'd be right in there, egging on whoever was at a disadvantage at the moment. But she felt surprisingly mellow and simply let it flow by. Soon Akbar joined in about his super-squad versus Krista's lame-ass crowd;

he'd beat her to the ridgeline by twenty minutes in a two-day battle. Ox rose to the challenge on that one and Krista still floated along.

"The joys of the season's first fire," she said softly to Evan.

He nodded, picked up one of his MREs and stabbed a plastic spork down into the pouch before leaning back against a rock and taking a mouthful. "First one always feels good. Mid-summer will be harsh and by fall it'll totally suck."

"'Bout right," she agreed.

"Can't wait."

Krista inspected him more carefully as he watched the fire. Every multi-season smokie jumped fire for a different reason, but if it really drove them, you could see the mark of it on their faces. Evan definitely had the mark, and not just of a multi-year jumper; every single person in MHA's crew had that. For Evan Greene it was something special, something deep drove him to the fire. Krista had seen that same look in the mirror her whole life.

Most guys, even most of the ones at MHA were gonna be gone after five or ten years in. Enough pain, enough broken relationships, a blown knee that surgery could no longer put back together, a broken back or worse—they'd be gone.

Akbar wouldn't. Two-Tall Tim had been a lifer—still was, just up in Alaska. Ox and Ant-man maybe. Nick the Greek would last this season, but probably not next.

Krista had found her dream career and would jump until they carried her out on a flaming backboard. And she suspected that Evan would also.

"Why did you cross over?"

"Well," Evan made his voice high and squeaky. "I was never happy as a woman and—"

A laugh burst out of her.

She almost snorted her mouthful of chili and beans—which really was a bit more palatable with the powdered hot chocolate though the barely rehydrated marshmallows that she hadn't picked out were a little strange. Evan might be many things, but he was about as male as she'd ever seen—transgender hung out nowhere near this boy-o.

"Why did you?" he asked her.

"Born this way, Soldier-boy."

"Yes, ma'am, Master Sergeant."

"It's not gonna stick, Rook. Give it up and try again."

# # #

"Hey, Great One," Evan shouted across the conversation to Akbar.

"What you want, Rook?" he called back.

Evan groaned.

Krista smirked at him and he ignored the fact that he felt some strange urge to kiss it off her face.

"Master Sergeant Krista claims not to have a tag. What's up with that?" Maybe he could get the group to pick up the theme.

"None of 'em stick," was all the help Akbar gave him.

"We tried, lord knows," Ox complained.

"They just slide off the woman," Nick the Greek replied. "They run away like the flames do when she faces down a fire. She don't even have to fight it when she's on a roll. Just glare and gone."

"Keep it up, though," Akbar offered cheerfully. "She might stick you with 'Rook' permanent-like which would be funny as hell."

"I'm so afraid," Evan did a woman-in-a-horror-movie voice.

Krista laughed beside him, which was the whole point. She had a damn fine laugh; it just wrapped around you and invited you in. Which only made him want to find more ways to bring it out.

Conversation turned, as it always did around post-jump campfires, to stories of bad burns. Later in the season it would turn into bad jumps that left a smokie injured or worse. Then burnovers. Though Evan had never been in one, he'd heard the stories and they sounded like true hell. After that it would get personal and Evan would once again have to fight against his inner demons. But tonight it was about triumphant firefights.

Krista kept her peace more than she joined in which didn't surprise Evan. She was like a mama hen watching over her chicks. "Mama Krista." It wasn't bad, but she was more than that too. He'd find it.

When questions of keeping watch on the fire arose, Evan volunteered for first shift. Lee the Ant-man raised a hand for who Evan should wake in two hours. Already, half the camp was asleep sitting up, but Evan was wide awake yet; as if sitting close beside Krista had electrified his system.

He went to the far side of the saddle and found an uncomfortable rock to sit on that offered him an excellent view over the firescape below but wouldn't let him sleep once the exhaustion slammed in. Smoke still climbed lazily upward in enough volume to shroud all but the brightest stars. Yet the smoke was thin enough that fire was no longer the only smell on the air. Small night breezes mixed in the scent of the conifer forest sleeping the night away to either side of the Black.

Below him, out in the Black, ranged dozens of small sporadic fires and minor flare-ups. The Hotshot crew had sacked out down by the stream, ready to hike back out as soon as the local cleanup team came in tomorrow to make sure the Black was truly dead.

There was a sudden flare-up, almost bright enough to read by for a moment. Deep in the Black, it soon settled due to a lack of fuel. From what Evan could see, this fire wasn't going anywhere.

"I always love this moment."

Evan spun around. He hadn't heard Krista's approach. His Special Forces senses had failed him; but they never failed him, even five years out of the service. Maybe she was military to move so stealthily. But he'd been so sure she wasn't.

Little more than a shadow, she settled onto the rock beside him.

"It is good," he spoke to cover his sudden unease. "When the battle has been won and the forest can lay down to sleep."

"Until the next fire."

"Until the next battle," he agreed. But there was a part of him that hated this too. An old part that ran far deeper— one thick with anger that rose up dark inside him and he was unable to avoid. He loved the adrenaline, the challenge, and the triumph. But he hated the aftermath even more than he hated the war.

He did his best to focus on Krista and the day's victory.

Focus on the positive, he reminded himself for all the good it ever did him.

They sat in an easy silence; easy despite another battle now raging inside him. The soft crackle of the distant flare-up the only sound in the night air. Even the night breeze had gone silent here with no leaves to whisper through.

From long practice he could normally shove the darkness, the anger aside. For some reason tonight it wasn't working. He hated the war in the Afghan Dustbowl where he'd spent five out of his six years in the service. So why had he signed up for the wildfire war at home? To avoid thinking about the past. He feared that internal darkness more than the enemy's bullet.

Say something, Ev. Anything.

"I crossed over from the Zulies because the winters were hard," he answered her earlier question, with a little too much truth. "I missed the fire," and the distraction of it. "MHA promised year-round action." And he did like the action.

"Might be hotshotting as a ground crew in Australia or jumping a fire in Argentina," Krista warned him from the dark. "But it does make the time flow by."

And just like that, it was as if she had understood why he'd entered firefighting in the first place, even though there was no way she could. He'd done his time in the Special Forces, lost good friends, good men to rag-head Taliban—and he'd be damned if he could figure out if the world was any better for all the blood they'd shed.

He'd gotten out when he no longer trusted himself to stay "on the reservation." There was a part of him that wanted to step out and just destroy the whole country, along with its innocents, in order to eradicate the fanatical infestation. He knew that was a bad headspace for a soldier with heavy weapons and command of a dozen-man Operational Detachment-Alpha team—a single Special Forces ODA could do some serious damage. When they tried to bump him to command of a full company of six ODA teams, he knew it was time for another career.

Now, as Krista had said, he was just letting time flow by. There had to be more than that. But he'd started to suspect there wasn't. And those long, dry winter months had not sat well with helping the time pass. The weight had grown on him. Now even these quiet moments between fires were becoming a burden.

He could feel her body heat close beside him despite the warmth of the night. Could feel a need in him for…

"Yes," she whispered from close beside him.

"Huh? What?"

"I been watching you, Rook."

He'd been watching her, too. And not just how she fought fire. He liked the way she commanded and the way she moved.

"You may love this moment, but you hate it too. Hate the waiting just like I do."

"I didn't say a goddamn word," he turned to face her, unnerved at how close that shot was to the mark. He hated the war but, someone help him, he loved the fight.

"Didn't need to," Krista's light eyes and hair caught the warm glow from the fire far below.

"You look…" like he needed his head examined. She moved like Special Forces, had the silence of one too. Not just Master

Sergeant, but also a multi-tour field grunt. How the hell did a civilian get like that? She looked like one of those Norse goddesses, the ones who wielded true power.

It's like she was custom made for him.

Well, he was about to get his ass kicked back to the Zulies, but that didn't stop what he did next.

He snagged a hand around her neck and kissed her, hard. He clenched his gut for the punch he deserved. But instead she returned his kiss with a heat that matched his own. Her tongue fought his as her own hand fisted in his short hair.

He was suddenly as eager and clumsy as a sixteen-year old boy from Boise getting his first kiss at the Turner Gulch boat ramp on Lucky Peak Lake. Some switch had been thrown and he was taking all the heat that Krista could give. Unaware of his own actions until they were complete, he grabbed one of her magnificent breasts, firm, lush, far more than a handful. Rather than pulling back, she leaned into his hold on her.

Evan shifted to nuzzle her neck—and instantly regretted it. Like all smokies after a fire, she had a band around her neck of sweat-dried ash and soot that had been ground into her skin by her shirt collar until it was a gray-black ring that tasted of salt and charcoal.

She laughed. It was a big hearty laugh for all that she kept it soft. He felt it move through her chest beneath his palm.

"Sorry," he hated himself for saying it. He pulled back and removed his hand from her breast. "I shouldn't have."

"Not in the Army anymore, Rookie."

"But you're still my comman—my boss."

"No, Akbar is. I'm just his jump partner. You want to go kissing him though, you'd better ask Laura first. She's pretty possessive about her man."

"I'll do that," he did his best to keep his tone dry. It still wasn't right the way he'd grabbed at her, driven at her. God, he wanted to throw her on the ground this instant and just bury himself in her until all of his black anger and pain was spent.

He'd tried that before, a long time ago. It hadn't turned out well. A two-month relationship hadn't made it to the first day of month three. He'd never figured out how to apologize for that one and then she'd been gone—with a real clear, *Don't you call me. Ever!*

"Just steer clear, Krista. I'm fine on a fire, it's just on the ground that I'm a mess."

She didn't respond for a long time and he couldn't turn to look at her. Couldn't face her because he didn't want to see the disgust on her face.

"Been a smokejumper ten years, Rookie. I live for messy."

Then she stood up, and did the craziest thing. She leaned down and gave him the softest kiss he'd ever had.

# # #

"Let me know when you're ready to wrestle some more," Krista whispered into his ear then started the hike back up over the rise to camp.

What the hell was that, girl? She never, ever kissed or slept with anyone on her team. It just made for an ungodly snarl. She'd watched other women try it, smokie or hotshot crew, and it always screwed up everything. Sometimes so bad that they bailed on the career 'cause it so messed with their heads.

But when Evan had unleashed that kiss on her, her brain had switched off and she'd finally figured out why she'd sent him on down the line that first day—the fourth reason. He didn't move or act like anyone she'd ever met in a decade of jumping fire. There was a barely contained power in him like a big blaze on the edge of blowup—that moment when forest fire became wildfire.

Besides, she'd never been kissed like that before in her life and she'd had some good ones over the years. He hadn't held back like she was some tender female, he'd gone at her like he wanted her any way he could get her.

She stood a long time in the shadows of the camp and stared down at the sleeping smokies by the light of the failing campfire.

Krista wished desperately that she didn't want him to try again.

Chapter 4

The next three fires, which hit back to back, Evan threw himself into the firefight. He'd seen what the MHA teams could do and he did everything in his power to make sure he fully integrated in—driving himself until he was nearly shattered with exhaustion.

He'd also made sure that he ended up on Akbar's teams whenever there was a split.

By the time they hit Day Five on the Deerness Fire in northern California, he'd been running at full tilt for over two weeks without a break; they all had. The Deerness finally laid down around midnight. Everyone had dropped where they stood and slept.

Now it was just coming up dawn. Clear of smoke, the pines of the Shasta-Trinity National Forest were a soft wonderland. The Black ranged across three ridges, but already deer and squirrel were nosing around the edges. A Steller's jay cocked its black crested crown at him to see if he had any food, then flitted off with a high-pitched *skreeka!* of disgust when he didn't make some offering.

"Tell me," Akbar waved him over to help ready the gear for pickup.

"Tell you what?" Evan knew exactly what, but he really didn't want to talk about it.

"Tell me why you're trying to kill yourself on the fire or I'll yank your rookie ass off the line. I can't have you endangering the team."

That shocked Evan upright. Not just off the team. Not just away from Krista.

But a *danger* to the team?

God, no!

That went against all his training both as a soldier and a firefighter.

"Fuck!" he dropped down to sit on a boulder at the edge of the stream where they'd been rolling up hoses—getting ready for the helicopter to airlift them back to the local airfield. *Not again!*

Akbar sat down beside him. He was a little man, a head shorter than Evan, but there was no question who ruled on a fire. There were jokes that he was a direct descendant of Agni, the Hindu god of fire. And knowing Akbar, he'd been the one to start the rumors because what did a bunch of Oregon smokies know from Hindu gods.

"You started clean," Akbar told him. "Damn good on the fire up by Mt. Rainier. Something happened there. You got even better, but you also got crazier. Now I know from crazy, jumped fire with TJ who wouldn't quit until a tree almost took him out after forty years as a smokie…and still he wanted back in. But you got some other-level shit going on."

Evan stared down at his blackened hands; soot ingrained in every pore and knuckle line despite wearing gloves. He felt sick to his stomach and cold with a sudden sweat that he'd be the one to put the team at risk.

"You aren't gone scary yet, Evan. But you gotta ease back. You keep driving like you are and you're gonna hurt yourself."

If he hurt himself, that would take others off the fire to assist him. If he hurt someone else in the process...

Unacceptable, soldier!

"I'll..." *what?* "Fix it, Akbar. Sorry to spook you."

"Long way from spooking me, Rookie," Akbar slapped his shoulder cheerfully. "Just consider this my early warning system. For spooky you gotta meet my wife," his laugh was always easy and twice his size. He went back to rolling hose.

"Unpredictable?" Evan struggled to catch his breath, to focus on something other than his one fear.

"Duh! Woman married me of all damn fool things to do." Akbar picked up the sixty-pound Mark III water pump as if it weighed nothing. He carried it to the stack of gear they'd been mounding near the helispot where an MHA helicopter would land to clear all of their equipment off the hillside. "She got me to stop dead in my tracks and never look back. If that ain't some kinda spooky magic, nothing is."

That wasn't the kind of problem Evan was having. He wasn't fighting his attraction to Krista. He was in pitched battle against bringing his shit into her world. That first taste of her had turned an idle curiosity into a heap of need that was fast burning up his insides.

Well, hiding sure as hell wasn't working. It was like he'd forgotten his training. Green Berets don't hide from problems, they fix 'em.

Time to fix this, Ev.

# # #

Krista sat on the floor, slouching against the rear bulkhead of the DC-3, and tried to let her body unwind. The return flight from the Deerness Fire to MHA's base up at Mount Hood was only about three hours. Most of the smokies had crashed into sleep the minute they were aboard, some stretched out on the floor, others atop lumpy piles of gear. That opened up enough of the sideways facing seats down one side of the hull for others to stretch out there.

Krista had landed sitting beside the jump door, and Evan against the back of the pilot's seat at the far end of the plane.

She'd considered being hurt, the way Evan had backed away from her. Considered it seriously even though she was so used to it. School dances, county fairs, boys never approaching her.

But then she'd watched how Evan Greene attacked the fire. This was a big, powerful man battling some serious issues. And she could only respect the way he did it, by working so damn hard that he was forcing other MHA crew to struggle to keep up.

It was kind of funny that maybe she'd so messed with a man's head that he was turning from a good firefighter into a great one. She didn't have that kind of effect on guys. They jumped her or she jumped them, they had a good time for as long as it lasted, and they were done.

But Evan had something else happening and she could tell it wasn't just about her, so she'd let it run a while.

He read fire as well as the next five-year smokie, but he fought it like only she and Akbar could—with a tireless efficiency that pushed right past physical limits as if they weren't even there. Probably his soldier training. Even Ox didn't have that level of discipline, he simply had such a deep capacity that he could keep up.

But whatever drove Evan, she was starting to be ticked that it seemed to be driving him away from her rather than towards.

Whatever demons were biting his ass didn't scare her, they were his demons after all, not hers. And, she had to admit to herself that she liked that about him. Johnny Q. Boring, Mr. Enlightened and well-rounded, "I know who I am," never did anything for her. Oh, they could be fun for a tumble; but the dark-and-broody soldier guy? That made Evan...interesting.

"He doesn't do something about it soon, I will," she muttered to herself.

"Ha!" Akbar had been slouched against the rear bulkhead close beside her, but she'd thought he was asleep. "That explains it."

"Explains what?" she knew her attempt to sound innocent was lame. She'd never gotten away with it before. She'd tried, like after gluing the school quarterback's locker shut with industrial adhesive from the auto shop, with the quarterback inside—in payment for how he was treating the cheerleaders. Rather than being thankful, they had all flocked to the jerk's defense. Then when they'd found out she'd been the one— real tough, she was the only person bigger than he was in the school and she'd been lousy at protesting her innocence—they'd ostracized her even more than she already was.

"No way," Akbar sounded totally pleased with himself. "I'm not copping on a bro, but now I get what's going on."

"Careful or I'll rename you Johnny the Dweeb and I'll make it stick." Her failed attempts to look away from the sleeping rookie wasn't helping her claims of innocence any.

"You can't," Akbar didn't sound the least worried. "It's my name."

"Soon to be Johnny the Dweeb," she threatened. But he was right. Johnny Akbar Jepps' middle name actually meant "great," so Akbar the Great was technically redundant. And he *was* a great firefighter even if he now owed her three beers for better parachute landings and she only owed him one.

"I can tell you this though," Akbar shifted into a more comfortable position and shut his eyes. "Only one way you're gonna find out what's driving him. Gotta get up close and personal for that, just like I did with Laura."

"You went after her like a lovesick bull calf."

"Yep," he agreed sleepily. "And look where it got me."

Krista considered the advice and decided it was one of the smarter things Akbar had ever said. She wasn't interested in anything permanent, but Evan Greene was one of those guys that was permanently interesting. She considered thanking Akbar, but his breathing had shifted into a soft snore.

He was smiling in his sleep.

Laura had definitely done something strange to him.

Chapter 5

*T*hey'd *left the Deerness* Fire shortly after dawn. From fire to airport by helo then DC-3 back to base.

Evan had brooded on Akbar's advice for the entire flight back and come to only one conclusion—he'd been a total chicken shit. No wonder he was feeling so pissed at the world; he wasn't being honest.

Fix that now, soldier. But circumstance didn't lend him any opportunity.

After landing on the grass-strip runway at the MHA base, they unloaded several tons of crap. Then everyone pitched in to clean, organize, repack chutes, and reset all of their gear into the speed racks. The base might be set up in an old, rundown boys' camp with a grass runway down the middle, but the gear was top flight and was always maintained in perfect condition first, no matter how tired they were.

Evan passed Krista half a hundred times, but she was always going the other way, or one of them was loaded down.

His frustration was climbing with each passage. The only way he was going to be able to fix the problem as he'd promised Akbar was to get Krista alone and apologize properly. And that just wasn't happening.

Then everyone hit the showers.

It was coming up noon by the time he was clean.

The guys got him to go back in to scrub off a missed spot on his back several times before he caught on that they were just messing with him. Damn it! He was even reacting like a rookie.

They got a good laugh and he felt even stupider than he already did.

In the Green Berets, SFG was supposed to stand for Special Forces Group, not for being such a Stupid Fucking Goon that you fell for every stupid ass…

He took a deep breath. Green Berets were the guys they sent to build peace in the villages and to build relationships to support the counter-insurgency; he'd been one of the very best at it. His ODA had ferreted out more terrorists than anyone except maybe Delta Force because of how smoothly they worked with the Afghan civilians.

And here he was wound up like an idiot…rookie!

He deserved the goddamn name.

Mark Henderson, the MHA Incident Commander, declared the rest of the day off. No fire calls until tomorrow. After fourteen days on fire, it wasn't very generous, but based on the cheers, the crews were psyched anyway. Everyone except for him. And he knew that was only because his mood sucked at the moment.

They stampeded to the parking lot and headed down into the town of Hood River perched on the edge of the Columbia Gorge. They were going to hit the Doghouse Inn, the smokejumper bar they'd introduced him to during training and try to pick up some windsurfers. It was a great dive, one of the best he'd ever been in, but he totally wasn't in the mood.

So he stood there and watched the gravel fly as battered pickups and over-powered muscle cars ripped out of the parking lot. He didn't know what Krista drove, but he stood there until the parking lot quieted and the first birds were daring to call out tentatively, testing the abrupt silence after the noontime mayhem.

He'd missed her again. Well, following her to the Doghouse was just going to place him in the same unmanageable crowd.

"Shit!" he muttered softly to himself, the calling bird, and anyone else who was listening.

He spun on his heel and walked smack into her. Krista had come up not two feet behind him wearing running shoes, worn jeans, and a stretched t-shirt that proclaimed, "Wildland firefighters do it in the wild."

"Goddamn it!" he stumbled back a step, then another. "How in the hell do you keep sneaking up on me?" And why was he yelling at the woman he'd just spent the entire flight trying to figure out how to talk rationally to.

"Hello yourself." She was smiling at him. "Pretty day, isn't it? How are you? Pissed at the universe? Really? What a shocker."

He growled. It was all he was capable of.

"So, why are you looking for me?"

"How did you…" Because he was that obvious. Evan closed his eyes and counted to ten. Then to twenty. He considered going for thirty but it wasn't helping.

He opened his eyes and she hadn't moved. Still had that smile that made her look so damn good, and like she knew shit that the rest of the universe didn't.

"Look, I'm sorry about—"

"Yeah, you said that before. Dumb thing to say. Try again."

He clenched his fists to try and keep still. To hold his focus. Clenched them until his fingers throbbed. Bore down as if he was lifting a heavy weight and…it wasn't doing any more good than the counting had.

Evan turned and walked off across the gravel parking lot. Maybe he'd just crawl into his Toyota pickup and drive back to Montana, see if he could still get a slot with the Zulies.

This time he heard her, trotting lightly over the gravel behind him, but making far less noise than she should in the process.

"Hey, Evan. Slow down there."

He walked past his truck. Maybe he'd just walk back to Montana. But when he hit the turn in the dirt road that led down the mountain, he walked straight across it into the trees. He'd always felt at home in the trees; something he'd missed desperately in Afghanistan. Even when they had forests there, they made no sense—thick holly and oak atop the ridges, and thinning down or gone in the desert-dry valleys.

A couple hundred yards downslope past the road he found a log. A big tree, a Doug fir that was a good four feet in diameter. It had toppled to the forest floor and buried itself halfway into the duff. Too weary to go further he sat and faced outward farther into the shadowy woods.

A small stream, probably glacier cold, ran nearby splashing brightly over stones and ducking under fallen tree limbs. It rested a brief time in a pool a dozen feet across, then continued on its way. Surrounding it were mature spruce and pin oak, no alder, a lot of detritus carpeting the ground; it had been a long time since there was a fire here.

He sat...and waited.

As silent as a deer, Krista moved up beside him and sat just a hand's breadth away.

He'd run dry. Had no idea what to say.

So he just sat.

# # #

Krista was puzzled by Evan. He wasn't just avoiding her. He was hurting, but not in any way she recognized.

So she sat on the log beside him and tried to puzzle it out.

When a rookie—a true rookie, not someone as massively skilled as Evan—couldn't break through on a new skill, they'd internalize it until it became a canker sore. If she couldn't find a way to dig it out or break through, the rookie was just gonna get stuck, maybe permanently.

Krista had also watched candidates make it through the entire training and then freeze at the door on their first fire jump after dozens of practice ones. Never get past it.

Or stand in front of their first big fire and get so hypnotized by the flames that they would have stood there gaping until the fire burned right over them.

But Evan wasn't like any of those, so Krista didn't even know where to begin to help. And she really did want to help. Maybe, for a change, she could stop teasing him and actually answer some of his questions.

"I grew up here," Krista finally spoke and it was hard.

There were memories she didn't want to relive because she couldn't get them back. Pop was gone and had taken all of the good memories with him.

"Not here, but in the forest. North of here. Pop built fine furniture using wood off the land. My first and best memories were tramping through the woods looking for just the right piece. Could take us days. Then when we found it, I'd run home and fetch Charlie, a big roan gelding. We'd drag the log back to this milling saw we had. Pop cut his own lumber, shaped and formed it. I was never much at woodworking, but I loved the forest and I could track down a good fall like nobody's business."

"That doesn't explain how you're so quiet in the woods?" His voice was rough when he finally spoke.

"We were pretty broke, so most of our food came from the forest. Pop was a felon, grand theft auto as a kid. Just some joy ride that crossed four state lines before he totaled the car. Law says felon equals no guns. We did bow hunting: deer, elk, got a bear once. Rabbit, even duck. I learned how to be silent there," that silence was something they shared.

And Krista loved the forest, could never get out in it enough. Didn't matter if they'd just spent a week or a month on a fire, she was always happiest walking beneath the trees.

"Where did you learn to be so damn quiet?" she asked him.

"Fort Bragg, North Carolina," his voice was still dull. Monotone. "And three consecutive tours overseas, long ones."

"Knew you were military, didn't know you drew that card."

"Volunteered. Special Forces. Green Beret."

Krista didn't know what to say. A number of boys from her high school had gone military to get out of Concrete. They'd all come back. A few in a box, most of the others just…changed and not all of those in a good way.

She inspected Evan's profile, but there was no clue there.

He continued to stare steadfastly straight ahead.

"Well, at least that explains why you're so damn good at what you do. You've definitely got the skills."

"Even if I don't have a name." There was a small spark of humor; the first she'd heard since the Mt. Rainier fire. She'd take that as a good sign.

"Haven't pinned you down yet, Rook."

His smile was perfunctory, his nod small, his gaze distant.

"But that's not what's eating at you. So what is?"

He just shook his head.

She hit him. She bunched her fist and drove it into his arm. Krista had leveled assholes in a bar with that blow, had taught the auto shop teacher exactly what you didn't do to high school girls. Taught him so well he'd left Concrete that night and never come back.

Evan had kissed her then avoided her. Fine. But he didn't get to ignore her when she was sitting right here.

Even as she fired off the blow, Evan snapped out a hand so fast that she couldn't see the move though she was looking right at him.

One moment she was millimeters from punching him hard enough to send him tumbling off the log.

The next, his massive hand was wrapped around her wrist. He didn't knock her blow aside, he simply absorbed the full force of it with that grab. Then he didn't lever her wrist to take her down, though she could feel just how effortlessly he could do that. She was strong, but he was in a whole other category.

"Sorry, reflexes." He held her wrist a second, maybe two, then let go.

"You've got a problem, Rook." She massaged her wrist, not that he'd hurt it, but rather to feel the impossible power and speed Evan had exhibited. She'd never seen anything like it. Of course she'd never met a six-year Special Forces vet before either.

"I got problems?" He nodded. "Yeah, I knew that much."

"If Akbar's right, the problem is me."

That got his attention.

He spun to look at her for the first time. His dark eyes had often tracked her from a distance. She could feel the heat of his look even when she was close against a fire. Now it was high noon and despite them sitting a hundred yards into thickly shadowed woods, his dark eyes were clear and bright as crystal. A shade of brown as beautiful as a hundred-year oak.

"Not you. God, Krista, not you. That's what I'm sorry for. The problem is all me."

Krista cricked her neck. Not her? Some part of her had *known* it was the too-tall, too-broad, too-strong girl. And a part of her that she'd thought had accepted that truth back in high school, still wallowed in humiliation deep down inside.

Not her?

Evan was sitting still once more, so perfectly that he almost disappeared into the forest right before her eyes. Except for those eyes. They might be the color of the forest, but they were so brilliant and so alive.

"Then what *is* the problem?"

# # #

Evan shook his head, "I'll be goddamned if I know. I'm just toxic. Someone as incredible as you should steer clear of me. Way clear. It's the best advice I've got for you. I'm sorry I made you think this was about you." Then he turned back to stare at the woods and the splashing stream.

He couldn't stand to keep looking at her. Maybe her life hadn't been idyllic, but he could hear her love of the time with her dad. She had more energy and passion than he'd ever have again. That much he'd left overseas with the bodies of too many friends. And before that…but he couldn't bear to think about that.

At least he'd said what needed to be said. As long as they didn't need to keep avoiding each other, he could face the fire. He'd just have to crank it down a notch or two. Keep his head in the game so that Akbar would know Evan could chill when he needed to.

He could feel Krista inspecting him, but knew he'd blown whatever chance they'd had.

It's never too late to come see us, Captain Greene, he could hear the voice of the Veteran Affairs counselor they'd made him visit as part of leaving the military.

But he wasn't one of those poor saps with PTSD. He'd been afraid that he might be, but when a tree had exploded right near him on his third fire, he hadn't descended into hysteria or terror. He hadn't revisited the battlefield in his mind except for a sharp bite of bitter adrenalin on his tongue. Sure he'd jumped plenty in surprise, but he hadn't known that a tree could explode from superheated sap with the force of a AT4 anti-tank round.

He was just—

Krista grabbed his face in both hands and kissed him hard.

"What the hell?" He managed to pull back.

She didn't say a word, instead she took up his right hand and unfolded it from the fist he'd unconsciously clenched it into.

He tried to help, but couldn't seem to connect willpower to hand muscles.

When she had it unfolded, she looked him square in the eye. There was mischief in those bright blues, but he couldn't make any sense of it.

# # #

Krista wasn't afraid of him. There wasn't a mean bone in his body, just some hurt ones.

Watching him sit there and fold up on himself, she no longer felt anger over him pushing her away after that first kiss, at avoiding her ever since, or even at assuming his apology covered the bases. All he'd done was show her what a good man he was, even if he didn't see it.

And then she'd known what she wanted.

She'd wanted to feel like she had when he'd first kissed her atop that ridge. She wanted to feel beautiful, though she knew she wasn't. She wanted to feel desired, which Evan clearly did. And—much to her surprise—she wanted Evan.

Krista wasn't big on denying herself.

So, she looked him right in the eyes, daring him to deny her. Then she placed his hand once more on her breast, exactly as it had been that night and leaned back in for the kiss she wanted.

Krista expected the attack, the hunger, the desperate need.

What she didn't expect was for him to kiss her eyelids closed. To cradle her breast in that powerful hand as if it was a rose. To brush his other hand into her hair and pull her close.

This time, when he nuzzled her neck, it wasn't thick with soot and sweat and it didn't make her laugh. It made her groan.

The world blurred, the forest became a swirl of bright sun and dim shadows beyond her closed eyelids. Flashes of green leaf and bark brown when she managed to open them, and Evan's eyes which had gone almost black.

But still he didn't rush, didn't grope or grab.

She'd have known what to do with that. Hold tight, drive hard, sweat, and be done.

When he pulled loose her shirt and bra he slowed to an excruciating pace, admiring, tasting, nuzzling until the cry that was forced out of her silenced the forest. Tenderness was not something any man brought to Krista; the power of it shocked her almost as deeply as the action itself.

Then her pants were gone, a moment she didn't remember. And his lips had traveled up her thigh, a series of moments she remembered perfectly, he groaned in turn.

"I need you, Krista. But I didn't bring any…"

Now it was her turn to lay a hand upon his lips. He might not have, but she knew what she'd gone hunting in the forest this day, even if this was more, so much more than she'd planned. She dug some protection out of her pants pocket and pressed it into his palm. Her need to feel him take her had grown until she was shuddering with it.

An easy tug peeled free his t-shirt, and he shucked his pants—a naked warrior god in the wilderness. She could see that his body was battered—he bore several scars, but it was also magnificent—powerful despite the damage. Perhaps more so specifically because it had survived the damage.

Then he lay her down on the forest floor upon their spread clothes, and finally he delivered what she'd expected. From the first moment he entered her, it was as if they'd both stepped into the middle of a fire.

The heat didn't spark, it flashed over. Like a wildfire at mid-afternoon, when the wind shifted and the air was so achingly dry that it ripped the moisture right out of the wood, a wild heat and energy blew up between them.

Evan drove at her, but no harder than she pressed up to meet him. He grabbed at her chest, drove her down with his mouth, and pinned her to the forest floor until she thought they might ignite it.

He swallowed her cries and she his when the out-of-control blaze scorched through their bodies. He drove her so far upward that all she could do was hang on and let him take all he needed.

With a final arching moan that ripped from deep in his body, he froze and then released in glorious pulses that sent her flying again.

They spun down from the sky, locked together, riding the twisting winds, until they finally landed so softly that she could easily cushion his final fall with her body. He lay upon her like a dead man, which was appropriate, for she lay like a spent woman.

"Damn, Rook. We strike fire like that, we must be doing something right."

Evan finally propped himself up on his elbows, but lifted no more than his head. "I'm on the verge of saying something stupid," his voice was a whisper as he inspected her reaction with those dark eyes and their secret depths.

"Then don't. Anytime you want to bring that much game to the firefight, I'll be ready for you."

# # #

Evan looked down at her and saw only a smile and those marvelous blue eyes that always smiled too. He'd wanted to use her and ended up being gentle instead. And then when he'd finally thought he'd be gentle, she had welcomed him in and he'd gone near to madness.

"In that case, I'll resist being as stupid as is my norm—"

"Yeah, right. I can see that stupid is one of your issues."

"—and I'll simply say that you're incredible."

"See," Krista wiggled beneath him with her legs still firmly clamped behind his butt, "not stupid at all."

A squirrel ran across the top of the log they now lay beside and paused to look down at two naked people wound tightly together before skittering along.

The type of women he'd always been attracted to, with their long legs and designer clothes, would never be caught making love where a squirrel could stop and observe. Instead he'd just screwed the living daylights out of a woman who—

With a twist of her hips, she flipped him onto his back, knocking loose a waft of rich pine and good soil from the forest floor. Last winter's leaves were soft beneath him and if the needles pricked a little, he didn't care.

"Now," she looked down at him. "Let's see just what we can do with this nice body of yours while it recovers."

He bore a dozen scars, bullet, knife, and fire and she didn't seem to care. Instead she took just as much time teasing and tasting as he had. Her hands were powerful but gentle as no lesser woman's had ever been, which only made her all the more impressive—all that strength ever-so carefully controlled.

By the time she was straddling him and his hands were once again filled with those amazing breasts, he didn't care about anything either, except making sure he could get more of this woman.

As she eventually eased her way over him, so slowly it was almost painful, he nudged at the darkness inside him. Except it wasn't there to nudge.

It had been a constant companion for so long that he knew it would be back. But finding freedom from it for even this one moment was enough to make the world shine.

But none of it shone like the woman moving over him, her fair skin dappled in sunlight and shadow, those blue eyes closed and her head thrown back as if she felt just as incredible as she looked.

Chapter 6

*W*e need calories," *Krista* groaned; groaned because she didn't want to leave their idyll in the woods.

"And sleep," Evan noted.

"Wish you hadn't said that." They'd been awake for most of the last three days except for the six hours between when the Deerness Fire lay down and the sun came up. Now she could feel every muscle sagging with weariness, both from the fire and from the unaccustomed, but very welcome exercise they had just performed.

"C'mon, Rook," she rolled to her feet and offered him a hand up.

That got a low laugh from him.

"See, Mama Krista got what it takes to cure them ills," she shook her hips like a belly dancer.

When she turned for her clothes he came up behind her and scooped his hands around and up over her breasts.

"Enough of that. We know what you like." But she did let herself lean back against him for a moment and simply enjoy his attention. He was an amazing lover. And so what if they were on the same smoke team; it wasn't really going to hurt anything if they had some fun for a while.

That didn't sound like her at all. She never…but oh god for the first time she wanted to.

No harm, no foul. Not if they kept it light? She hoped so because she was past caring about that.

When he started in on more than her breasts and she could feel him recovering where he pressed against her, she brushed his hands aside and stepped out of reach.

"Get dressed, now."

"Yes, Master Sergeant!" He snapped to attention and saluted her. And his hand wasn't the only thing saluting.

"You are going to be so much fun, Rook. I'm looking forward to it."

And she was. Far more than was usual for her. He was funny, when he wasn't doing his dark-and-foul-mood macho thing. And he was built to order for her body. Even the men who were her height were often of a lighter build. Evan was big and solid enough to make her feel feminine, which was definitely a new experience.

She waited until she had her shoes laced and he was still missing one shoe and his shirt.

"Race you to the mess hall, Rook. First one in gets pick of the fridge."

"Sure thing, just give me a sec," he bent down and tugged on his other shoe.

Krista placed a hand atop his head and shoved hard.

He tumbled backward, letting it turn into a roll and landed back on his feet. He glared up at her. The cool move was ruined by all of the dead needles and bits stuck in his dark hair.

She bolted before he could recover.

She dove over the log they'd started out sitting on, did a tuck and roll like a parachute landing, and came back to her feet at a run. Not just some mile-eater of a smokie trot…

A bark of laughter sounded behind her—well behind her, but she bet that its owner wouldn't remain far back for long.

…instead she went for an escaping-a-runaway-fire sprint.

# # #

Evan scooped his shirt, stuffed it down in his waistband and vaulted over the big log as if it was a gymnast's pommel horse.

He caught only flashes of her golden hair through the thick underbrush as he ducked under branches and dodged blackberry patches. He hadn't run into them coming out, so she must know about them and was trying to lead him into their clutching thorns.

This wasn't a Green Beret operation and he wasn't wearing full battle gear. So, to protect his bare chest, he lost time dodging around the wide, prickly bushes and still earned a few scratches from far-arching branches he didn't spot in time.

She had a hundred feet on him when they hit the road.

Seventy-five at the parking lot.

He dug in until he was spitting gravel from beneath his sneakers just as the departing muscle cars had earlier.

Krista still had him by fifty feet at the far side of the lot as they crossed into the compound. Damn but she was a magnificent runner. Her legs were long, but there wasn't a thing frail about them. They were powerhouses that delivered immense speed.

Up between the weathered-shingle bunkhouses on the left and the back of the kitchen on the right. At the battered picnic tables where MHA ate meals when at camp, Krista ran down the length before taking a sharp turn toward the kitchen door.

In a last effort to beat her, Evan turned at the same moment she did, taking a diagonal path. He used a bench to jump up to the tabletops and ran over them like rough terrain—bench, tabletop, bench, ground, bench, tabletop—up and down, up and down.

Wildfire on the Skagit

She hammered through the door two steps ahead of him and managed to slam it in his face. Unable to stop, he crashed into it full force, only thinking to turn a shoulder at the last moment.

# # #

The heavy wooden door blew off its hinges with a *crack* as loud as a falling snag.

Krista barely managed to dodge aside as Evan crashed through.

The door landed flat onto the concrete floor and Evan tumbled into the cramped dining room where they ate when it was too cold or wet to eat out at the picnic tables.

He rolled twice before fetching up against a stack of folding metal chairs. They scattered to the floor with such a crash she had to cover her ears for several seconds and still her ears hurt.

Impossibly, he came out of it in a low crouch poised in what looked like some kind of martial arts stance. Soldier trained.

"Real smooth, Rook," Krista managed it with a straight face. The doorframe was shredded, the door on the floor was badly cracked, and metal chairs were scattered every which way throughout the room. Crouched in the middle of it was a gorgeous piece of soldier bleeding from a half dozen scratches.

He grinned up at her, "Green Berets are known for their grace and delicacy."

For half a second she considered being insulted, those two adjectives had certainly been aimed at her as weapons many times in her past. But she couldn't deny his grin and burst out laughing.

They both lost it and were soon both holding their sides at the pain of the laughter.

As promised, once they'd recovered their sanity, he gave her victor's choice of the leftovers. They were back in the kitchen—she wolfing down some cold spaghetti and meatballs, Evan with a massive meatloaf sandwich of bread-meatloaf-bread—no stopping for any fixings—when a shout sounded from the main door.

Krista peeked out and saw Betsy standing in the shattered doorway, fists on her hips.

"What the hell have you done to my dining room?"

Krista started heading for the back door with bowl and fork in hand, but Evan blocked her way. "Can't go dodging your deeds, Mama Krista."

Betsy stalked into the kitchen. She might be barely five-six of lean redhead, but she ruled the kitchen and hence the stomachs and hearts of all of MHA's smokies.

"Krista! What the hell?" Betsy waved a hand toward her shattered dining room.

Think fast! Gotta be a way out of this.

Krista turned and pointed at Evan.

"He did it!"

Chapter 7

*T*he Tillamook Hill Fire led to the Reno Creek Fire, and then a trio of brutal burns down in Southern California.

Downtime wasn't an issue—they had none. So Evan didn't have any trouble keeping his focus on the fire.

However, not having any downtime was becoming a serious issue for other reasons.

You aren't seventeen, Ev! That year he'd graduated high school and signed up for Army ROTC at Boise State. He'd only gone ROTC because he'd burn in hell before giving his parents the "we paid for you schooling" weapon to add to their arsenal.

No, he was thirty-two this fall, but he wanted to be playing grab-ass with a hot woman as if he was still a teenager. There was a major problem here in his libido's opinion. In truth, they didn't get a single second of time together, because you sure didn't play games while on the fire.

Their time off mainly consisted of passed out on the jump plane in transit between fires, or passed out coyote fashion on a fire. He didn't care if MHA paid a bonus for wrapping himself in a tarp and sleeping where he fell rather than a crappy tent in the middle of a noisy fire camp, it didn't get him a single moment more with Krista.

The only slow times were meals, and on these fires, a number of those had been eaten while trooping from one fireline to the next wearing sixty pounds of gear.

"Goddamn it, Akbar," he complained as good-naturedly as he could while they crawled onto yet another flight in full gear. "Don't you guys ever get off the fireline?"

The engines on the DC-3 roared to life filling the cabin with a healthy dose of hot engine stink before they could shut the rear door.

"Rook is whining!" Akbar called out to the rest of the plane as soon as the engine noise had been mostly shut outside. "Wants a day off when there's fires burning."

Calls of "Wimp!" and similar were shouted by the others. Even Krista joined in with a loud raspberry noise.

"Quality of rookies these days is sad state of affairs," Ox offered in his deep voice, sounding more like a Baptist minister than a Russian strongman.

"Shit you guys, you know the NASA line: *On Earth...*"

Everyone on the DC-3 joined in, "*Something is always burning.*"

Evan turned to Akbar and held out his hands, palm up. "See?"

"True. True," Akbar nodded sagely but by the look in his eye, Evan had just made another rookie mistake.

"What?"

Akbar glanced over at Krista who nodded. Then Akbar looked up the plane's aisle and shouted over the sudden roar of the engines cranking up to launch them down the runway.

"Ox!"

"Yeah, boss!"

"Next week you'll be promoted to my jump partner for a few days. Rook wants your slot."

"Hallelujah!" Ox fist pumped.

"What?" Evan had missed something and his jump partner was ecstatic about it.

Akbar simply patted him on the shoulder.

Evan looked at Krista for a clue. She didn't say a word, but she was grinning like a lunatic. Clearly he'd not only stepped in it, but stepped in it deep.

No amount of hounding Akbar or Krista over the next seven days gained him a single hint.

All Ox, the asshole, offered was a chilling laugh and a darkly muttered, "Doom! Doom!"

# # #

Finally off the fires, Evan got to sleep in a bed. Not with Krista, but he was past caring. The bunk was heaven.

They'd all unloaded, restaged the gear, and crawled into the showers then their bunks. No calls of "Doghouse Inn!" Not many even made it down the buffet line that Betsy somehow managed to drag together despite following the MHA flight crews from camp to camp with her cook tent and supplies in tow.

Three straight weeks on fires equaled severe sleep deprivation.

Evan managed to resurface by midday, sixteen hours later. He felt so much better, except for the permanent kink in his neck from sleeping the whole time in one position.

He went out in front of the bunk house and, blinking at the late morning sunlight like an owl, started doing some stretches.

"Hey, Rook!"

"Hey, Master Sergeant!" Gods but she looked fantastic. "Damn but that smile of yours is a pleasure to wake up to."

Her smile got even bigger.

"We first up?" The camp was quiet; silent enough for a family of deer to be browsing the other side of the air strip along the line of MHA's jump planes and helicopters.

"Been up for hours, Rook. You're about the last one out of the sack. Everyone else is down at the Doghouse for lunch."

"Sounds great! Let's go. I could eat a horse or one of those deer; got your bow and arrow handy?" He always lost ten or fifteen pounds each fire season because it was impossible to consume as many calories as he was burning. He felt at least five thousand shy at the moment. Evan started moving in on her wondering if he could get a treat before they ate.

Krista pushed him aside, but not before he got in a nice kiss and a quick feel. "Go see if you can beg breakfast from Betsy."

Getting some calories and dragging Krista back into the woods on a beautiful summer's day sounded like a great idea. He headed for the kitchen to see if Betsy had forgiven him for shattering her door.

"And Rook?" she called when he was halfway there.

"Yeah?"

"Eat fast."

Didn't have to tell him twice.

# # #

Ten minutes and only a bit of a groveling for forgiveness later, he was back out at one of the picnic tables with a pair of monster burgers, all the trimmings, and a mug of black coffee that had never been near an Army coffee urn. It must be in some manual somewhere that all Army coffee was required to be served well burnt or maybe the urns were simply all set to stun. Betsy used Honduran beans and a smooth Italian roast for MHA's signature fare. Totally awesome. Another nice MHA bonus.

As for bonuses, Krista sat down across from him as he ate. Not at the same table so that he could play footsie with her, but instead leaning back against the next table over with her feet propped on the other bench of his table. It let him truly admire the woman.

Jeans, sneakers, a black t-shirt with a simple "Smokejumper" stretched wide across. Dark shades hid the blue eyes. Her smile was up to something and he couldn't wait to find out what it was.

"You make me wonder what I ever saw in other women."

"Are you like Ox? Want your women pixie sized?"

"Nope," he bit into his second burger and continued admiring her. "Always liked 'em long, just never thought about one who could keep up with me."

"Oh, I'm way ahead of you, Rook."

"How's that?"

"Told you to eat fast. Too late now," and Krista pointed toward the parking lot.

Evan took another bite of his burger and turned to follow where she pointed. Nothing there. He was about to turn back when he picked up the sound of a big diesel engine changing gears, downshifting for the steep final climb up into the parking lot. Truck-sized. No, his Army training adjusted the assessment even as he made it. Bus-sized. Different timbre to the exhaust.

In a dust cloud, a yellow school bus crested the dirt road and swung into the lot. On the side were the words "Hood River High School." On the display over the windshield it just said "Special."

"What the—"

"You wanted off the jump line, Rook. You got it."

The bus wheezed to a halt and the engine rattled to a stop.

"Mount Hood Aviation Smokejumper Camp for girls. We do this every summer."

He'd known she and Akbar were up to something with how affable they were being about everything, but this was way the hell out of bounds. Ox's "Hallelujah" was explained and Evan was so screwed.

Girls began climbing off the bus. High school ones that even at this distance he could see were armed with smart phones and attitude.

"What's this got to do with getting a break?"

Krista was on her feet. "Akbar never said a word about getting a break. C'mon, Rook. Time to meet our students." She slapped him hard enough on the shoulder that he almost inhaled the final bite of his burger.

Evan took a slug of his coffee and grabbed a fistful of French fries before tossing the rest in a garbage can and hustling after Krista. He pulled up alongside her just before she reached the kids.

"How many hours?" he whispered around a mouthful of fries and almost choked himself.

Krista just flashed that killer smile at him and turned away to face the twenty-plus girls and two parent chaperones who had piled off the bus. All sizes and shapes, shy and confident, chic and scruffy.

"Hey, girls," Krista waved merrily. "Welcome to Mount Hood Aviation's smokejumper and helibase. Hope you like the outdoors because we've got three days of fun planned for you."

"Thr—" was all Evan managed. He really did choke this time.

Krista thumped him on the back, hard enough that he almost spit the last of his fries on the kids.

"I'm Krista."

She aimed a thumb in his direction as he struggled to recover his composure.

"You can just call him Rook."

# # #

Krista had started the whole camp idea three years before. She'd thought about how much she loved the outdoors and even though Concrete, Washington was a town of less than a thousand in the middle of the Cascade Mountains, almost none of the girls got out in nature.

Boys went into the woods: deer hunting with their dads, trouble hunting with their buddies.

Girls didn't do squat. A dozen years ago, they were still expected to do bake sales and car washes to support the sports teams. She hadn't done anything about it then, but now she could.

The kids down in Hood River lived in an outdoor paradise but rarely thought beyond the windsurfing in the Columbia Gorge. When she floated the idea, she'd been given full support by MHA. She and Akbar had designed the camp and it was now a major hit with the high school girls.

While they were unloading their gear from the bus, Evan pulled her aside.

"What the—" he clamped down on the curse word and glanced over toward the school bus.

"Takes two to run the exercises safely," she offered in her sweetest voice.

His look of abject panic was simply too splendid and she couldn't stop goosing it.

"We take them out wilderness hiking and camping. Clear some line, teach them chainsaw technique. Then run them through the basic parachute trainer. Helicopter ride at the end if there are any helos not out on a fire. This year I even got them coupons for a free tandem parachute jump just south of Portland in case anyone wants to go. Two nights camping wild with the girls; it'll be great."

"Those are teenage girls." He sounded horrified.

"They are, Rook. I found out that some of them pay better attention if we have a macho smokejumper in the mix."

"Is this what Ox was being so damned happy about all week?"

"Ox was going to help this year, but you volunteered."

"I didn't— Well, crap, I didn't mean to."

"You want some together time, this is where I'm going to be." Krista suddenly cared about his answer to that. Which was unexpected. Since when did she care what a guy did or didn't do?

But before she could really worry at that, he grinned at her.

"Okay, that sold me. But I still think I was shanghaied."

"You were, Rook," and Krista couldn't stop the happy feeling inside that bubbled up at his easy acceptance.

"Can we at least—"

"Nope!" Damn but he was fun to mess with. "You don't get off the hook that easy. Rook is how you've been introduced, Rook is what you're stuck with."

He rolled his eyes at her, but followed her forward cheerfully enough when she waved everyone over toward the picnic tables.

# # #

"All electronics: cell phones, watches, music players, tablets," Krista told the round-eyed girls. "They all go in the bag."

Evan was handing out drawstring bags with blank name tags to the girls who sat scattered among Betsy's picnic tables.

"You gotta be kidding me!" More than one protested.

Evan did his best not to laugh in the girls' faces. "Your next charger is three days away," he spoke up in support of Krista. "And on a fire, we're pretty remote, so there are almost never cell towers."

"Solar charger, duh!" Two girls held up small panels. "Gotta have my music."

"Those go in the bag too," Krista informed them. "Nature is providing the soundtrack."

"Everything you want to have with you," Evan pointed to a line of rucksacks, "you have to carry in your own backpack for the next three days."

That certainly changed the dynamic. Within minutes, extra shoes, makeup, a couple of hairdryers, e-readers and books, and a surprising volume of extra clothes had all been transferred into the drawstring bags. It was hard for a guy to keep a straight face while watching such antics, so he did his best to look elsewhere.

Looking at Krista wasn't doing him the least bit of good. She was clearly used to this and enjoying his fish-out-of-water state far too much; something he'd definitely be paying her back for later. Looking at Krista also made him think other thoughts. He'd never understood those guys who liked younger women. Sure, they were great to look at, so perfect in youth. But the contrast of a woman like Krista, strong, confident, mature, and attractive as all hell put the girls to shame. Except these weren't girls, these were young women.

Evan had never been comfortable around teenage girls, well, not since he'd been chasing them as a teen himself. Now he couldn't help but see parts of his younger sister in each one and had to force that away and out of his mind.

Fast.

Down that path lay the ultimate black hole of his life.

He started trying to catalog them; they'd be less scary that way.

There was the really fit blond wearing the nametag Ash, obviously the top athlete of the group, quiet and focused.

Callie who was like a short, brunette Krista, solid and with a ready laugh.

Mallory, easily the prettiest of them all, was as concerned with her clothes and looks (one of the hairdryers came out of her gear) as with her status among the other girls. She also had a fragility that she was struggling to keep hidden behind a carefully studied perfection and a somber expression.

A fragility that was all too familiar and he looked away quickly.

Reena with the thick Mexican dark curls was another athlete—Ash's dark twin. They clearly hung together.

He could already see the groupings, but they were more bonded as a whole than he expected. No queen bee bent on controlling and manipulating those around her which surprised him.

"So, what's the common theme here?" the words were out before he realized that maybe showing his ignorance this early on wasn't the best idea.

"We're all amazing, Rook!" Callie called out. "Is that really your name?"

"Means 'rookie,' space case. He's a newbie," a black girl tagged as Nikkya responded.

Evan couldn't even find the voice to protest as the other girls laughed and joined in. The dynamics in his high school had been harsh and intensely cliquish. You were either in or out; and if you were "out," like his sister Francine, the gods themselves couldn't help you.

We're all amazing? Did they have any idea how...amazing that simple statement made them? He actually hoped not. Wouldn't it be incredible if they went out into the world actually believing that about themselves? *Look out, boys,* he mentally warned his younger gender mates.

"Outdoors Club," Ash said matter-of-factly. She'd had nothing to repack, had brought exactly what was on the list. So while the others fussed, she'd been doing leg stretches with her heel propped up on one of the picnic tables. Reena joined her, doing the same.

"What do you guys do when you aren't hanging out with smokejumpers?" That earned him a couple of appraising looks. His time in bars had taught him plenty about the power that the word "smokejumper" had over women, but it was weird to see it already manifested in several of the young girls. He made a mental note to stick close to Krista for self-defense.

"Trail runs," Callie pointed toward Ash and Reena and groaned as did several others in the group. "They're the queens of cross-country and keep trying to get us to go along. So not."

"Hey, Lee goes with us."

"I do, but I'd rather ride a bicycle any day," a tall girl with black hair down her back said. Her powerful legs displayed by her tight leggings said that cycling was indeed her sport.

"Windsurf," Meaghan piped up, a lively redhead. That received near universal smiles of acknowledgement from the others. Evan suspected that she was notoriously rabid about her preferred sport.

They continued around and Evan could start to see the pattern. They were the outdoorsy set from their school, but they approached it as if it was foreign land. They did things outdoors, but none of them had ever camped further out than a state park. Definitely none had loaded up a pack and gone tramping out into the wild with a bivy bag and a week's supply of food.

He'd done that all the time as a kid. He'd never really thought about why, it was simply where he was most comfortable. Why? Now that he thought about it, it was totally obvious: to get as far away from his dysfunctional, alcoholic, back-biting parents as possible.

He had incorporated wilderness survival techniques deep into his skill set long before the Green Berets had started filling in the blanks. He hadn't ever hunted with bow and arrow like Krista, but he'd been a dead shot with his .30-30 Winchester 94 with a peep sight by freshman year of high school. Mostly target shooting, but he'd often lived wild for weeks at a time with little more than a tarp and his beloved rifle. When the Special Forces had given him a telescopic sight, he'd become one of the top shooters in his whole company.

None of these girls had done that. He wanted to take them out and show them. Teach them that there was more to the outdoors than mandated sports. You could live quite comfortably out there if you needed to, even in modern times.

Krista knew that.

Maybe he was beginning to understand what she was trying to do here...but he'd still rather have gotten her off alone somewhere.

Not gonna happen, Ev, so dig in.

He gathered up a stack of hardhats and plopped one down on Callie's head.

"Hey!"

"Branch!" He called, then smacked her hat hard with another of the hats. The loud Klonk! grabbed everyone's attention. "Hurt much?" Evan did his best to make it a sneer as if she'd be a weakling to admit anything.

"Only my ears," Callie grinned up at him from under the brim.

"Someone yells *branch,* don't look up or you'll get it in the face," he nodded to her that she'd done good. "Fit the straps. The forehead band should be just snug enough that it doesn't come off if you're nodding in answer to a question. The chin strap loose enough that you can shout without choking yourself. Once you have it adjusted, you can tie it to the outside of your pack for later." And he began handing them out to the rest of the girls.

The two adults had hung in the background watching the goings on. He almost handed a bag of sunglasses to the woman to distribute—petite enough that she was definitely Ox's type. Catching himself on the verge of reinforcing stereotypes that he guessed Krista was fighting against, he handed them to the guy, Mac by his nametag, who looked like a gym teacher. "English lit," he introduced himself with a good strong handshake which Evan returned.

"These have laminate lenses," Evan announced loudly enough for all to hear. "Normal sunglasses can shatter if hit wrong, these won't. Civilian sunglasses go into your leave-behind bags."

Zelda, who introduced herself as "wife of the professor and cross-country coach,"—*the pixie was the athlete; so much for stereotypes*—he pointed toward the stack of Pulaski fire axes. "Each person gets one. You too." She laughed and headed to the stack of well-used tools and began handing them out.

Krista had been flipping through the paperwork on each girl, "Three vegetarians. Does raw elk meat count as vegetarian?"

It earned her a chorus of "Ewws."

Krista began handing around MREs to add to their packs.

"Now that's just plain cruel," he whispered when she passed close enough to smell her. He tried to turn off his nose, but it had clearly decided that Krista and heaven smelled much the same.

"How little you know me, Rook," and she moved on before he could think up a decent reply. She was right, but it wasn't for lack of trying. It had been a lack of time and the start of a bad fire season.

He handed out hunting knives with appropriate warnings about how to handle a long blade and instruction on how to strap the sheath to their thighs. Krista demonstrated how to open an MRE and how the heater worked to cook a meal in the outdoors. By the time she'd talked them through electrolytes and staying hydrated, Evan's stomach was getting up to a decent grumble.

He could see a couple of the thinner girls were already suffering from fading attention due to blood sugar crash.

He started to ask Krista about breaking for lunch when he noticed something was wrong. The girls were covering their ears though he didn't hear a thing over their talk back and forth. He only had a moment to register that Krista was smiling and looking just over his shoulder—

An air horn unleashed its unholy howl about two steps behind him.

Evan yelped in surprise and dove aside, sending bursts of laughter through the assembly. Everyone else had seen what he hadn't, Betsy coming up close behind him to announce lunch. Usually she just used an old fire engine bell mounted on the doorframe of the kitchen, but when the wind was high or the field was busy, she used an air horn so that anyone still in the bunks, working in the parachute loft, or across the field by the aircraft would know it was mealtime. Not close enough to hurt his ears, but more than enough to scare the crap out of him.

"Nice," he looked up at her from where he'd taken cover under one of the tables close by Mac's feet.

"Don't you be busting down my door anymore, Rook," and she stalked away but couldn't quite hide the smile. He guessed they were even now. He hoped to god they were.

Krista offered him a hand up, "Never mess with a Mount Hood Aviation woman, Rook."

"Yes, ma'am, Queen Smokie," he regained his feet and saluted.

But even as he said it, he knew that one wouldn't stick either.

# # #

Krista hadn't much chance to see Evan function in the wild, except on a fire. But she couldn't help but be impressed from the first moment. He wasn't merely at ease in the instructor position, he was skilled enough that those around him were at ease as well.

After lunch he took the back-of-the-group position, usually the most dreaded. There were always a couple of the kids who were simply overwhelmed by the true forest, and it would be up to the tail-man to keep them moving along. That took a special understanding right there.

Krista hiked across the airfield, past the two jump planes, Mark's Incident Command twin-prop Beechcraft, and aimed for the trailhead behind the row of the six helicopters.

"Hey, can't we go in one of those?" "That would be so cool."

"We are not that lazy," Krista told them.

"I am!" Callie raised her hand.

"Me too!" several of the others joined in. There had been a lot of surprise when they'd hauled on their packs, each weighing twenty-five pounds. Then Evan had told them that a smokie often carried sixty. With that deep voice and powerful demeanor of his, the girls had quieted much faster than normal. He'd already done better than any of the other smokies and they'd barely started. She and Evan carried significantly more gear, medical gear and radios, but their packs were still lighter than they usually carried to the line.

Krista let them stop and gather round her. She patted the nose of *Firehawk 03,* one of the three big converted Black Hawk helicopters, gloss black with a racing-car-flame paint job. They were amazing warhorses that had deeply changed the raw power MHA could bring to the fight.

"I'll tell you a secret though," Krista lowered her voice to entice them closer.

All of the girls leaned forward in anticipation.

"Our senior pilot, two others, and both of our mechanics are women."

"Whoa!" That woke a real buzz among them.

"I should point out," Evan raised his voice to cut through the excitement. "Three of the pilots, both of the jump plane pilots, and our Incident Commander are all guys."

"Pure luck," Krista raised her voice.

"Yeah!" "Pipe down in the cheap seats back there."

By Evan's easy smile, she could see that he too appreciated their responses as if she needed another reason to like him. They'd barely started and already the world of possibilities were opening up before these girls.

Her only problem with Evan had been that they weren't getting any of the alone time that her body was craving.

But *now* she was starting to wonder if that was the least of her problems.

She was also discovering the man behind the body and liking everything she found there…really liking it, which wasn't any version of Krista that she was familiar with.

She turned and led the girls off the far end of the airfield and into the Mount Hood National Forest along an old fireroad, leaving Evan to bring up the rear.

# # #

The first hour went pretty smoothly. These girls were tough and Evan was impressed.

Ash and Reena were real standouts, as he'd expect from their cross-country background, but most of the others were pushing right along with them.

Krista started teaching them wildlife: black squirrels, Steller's jays, a turkey vulture who inspected them from high above a small clearing, as well as how to tell the tree species apart. They were eating that up too.

He intentionally lagged behind so that the girls didn't feel pressured. If it had been his ODA out on a run or a fire team of actual rookies in testing, he'd be hounding their heels, pushing them to keep up. He wanted these girls to enjoy the experience. By moving a little slower, he gave them permission to move at a more sedate pace than the one Krista set.

He wasn't too surprised when Mallory ended up at the back of the pack. He cast a glance forward just to make sure one of the chaperones was in easy range, just in case the group's beauty queen had something on her mind that he didn't want to deal with.

But still he wasn't ready for the question when it came.

"Are you a soldier?"

Mallory's beauty pageant face didn't have the prerequisite smile anywhere to be seen. Instead, he was facing the frail girl he'd spotted behind the studied veneer.

"I was. I guess it still shows."

She nodded, "I recognized the training when you were fooling around with Krista."

"Do you have someone who's in?"

She folded her arms tightly as they walked as if she was chilled rather than sweating on the warm summer day. She finally managed a tight nod and a whisper soft, "I did."

Oh crap! There was all sorts of counseling for vets having a hard time—even the ones like him who didn't want it. But so little for their families.

He was trying to think of how to ask the next question, when redheaded Meaghan—who'd been at the tail end of the main group—dropped to one knee and studied something alongside the trail.

He and Mallory caught up to her quickly.

"What's that?" Meaghan was at the side of the trail by a spot that hadn't been trampled by the others' passage.

"Deer scat," Evan picked up branch to flick aside a few of the leaves that partially covered the pile; glad for the subject change.

Chicken? Beautiful girl with hard questions. Damn straight he was chicken!

"Small brown pellet poop from such a big animal always seemed weird to me."

Out of the corner of his eye he tried to gauge Mallory's condition. She looked okay, just…hard.

"It's only about twice the size of what a rabbit leaves behind. But bunny poop is always round. Deer, elk, and moose are oblong with no pinch off. At least three days old by the color." He poked a couple with his stick and they powdered. "More like a week by how dry they are."

"You know a lot about poop," Meaghan eyed him with amusement. But there was something else going on there that he wasn't sure how to read. She'd already known it was deer scat, but he played along.

"Occupational hazard. You want to recognize bear poop when you see it. Or wolf. We don't get wolves around here, but I've certainly jumped fires with them close by. They won't attack a human unless they're panicked; fire does that to them though, especially if they have young in a threatened den."

"Cool!" And then Meaghan rose to her feet so that she landed between Evan and Mallory. Was the redhead the one who would be causing him trouble? Had she used the excuse of deer scat to horn in on a misperception of why Mallory had slowed down to be with him?

Then she looped an arm through Mallory's. "C'mon, Mal. Let's hunt up more poop for him to tell us about," and led her ahead into the gap between him and the main group. But they weren't looking at the trail. He got the impression that Mallory wasn't looking at much of anything as Meaghan guided her around ruts and over fallen branches.

Another shift in what he was seeing. Meaghan had known Mallory was having a hard time with something, so she was being a friend, trying to make it easier. Of course. A fellow student would know the whole story.

Watching them together, taking care of each other, reminded him of wildfire teams and Special Forces ODAs...and not at all of Evan James Greene.

Because the one time it really truly mattered, he had totally failed.

# # #

Krista had pushed them steadily through the afternoon with only short breaks. It took four hours to reach the clearing she'd chosen for camp. It would have been an easy hike for any of these girls with the shape they were in...if they hadn't been loaded with twenty-five pounds apiece. She wanted them to hurt a little, but not too much.

"Great! Now, drop your packs and grab gloves and your Pulaski. Tina, stop using your sunglasses to keep your hair in place and pull them down."

She soon had them organized in the center of the clearing and was giving them techniques for cutting a line and how to use the hoe side of the Pulaski to cut through and peel back sod. Once that was peeled back, she showed them how to judge organic and inorganic layers.

"Clear me a circle. Mineral soils only for a six-foot diameter circle. Then peel back the top layer of organics for another four feet all around. Go."

That was when she noticed that Evan wasn't there. He was standing at the entry to the clearing, still wearing his full pack. She knew that look now; didn't know the root of it, but couldn't miss it. It hung like a personal shroud of darkness, looming over his head.

Krista double checked that the girls and the two chaperones were doing okay. And they were; chatting together, figuring out how to work closely together to achieve a common end.

She strode over to Evan, half afraid he would bolt and run back to camp.

He offered her a nod of recognition, but there was none of the heat coming off him like there had been all morning.

She simply scooped his arm in one of hers, spun him about, and walked him right back into the woods. She didn't stop until they were around the first curve in the trail and couldn't be seen or easily overheard.

"Evan."

"Yeah?" He didn't even know he was in some kind of weird space, but his eyes weren't focusing on her.

"If I were to shout *fire,* would you be okay?"

"Sure, I'd—" then he shook himself like a wet dog and rubbed a hand over his face. "Oh crap! I'm sorry, Krista. Yeah, I'm fine. Didn't even know I'd—"

He didn't finish, but she knew he'd gone back to the dark place down inside him. That he'd gone there despite the supercharge of the young women's excitement practically making the air around them vibrate worried her.

"Straight up, Evan. Do I need to send you back?"

That brought his attention into sharp focus. "No, Krista. Sorry. I'll be fine."

"My girls are safe around you?"

"I swear. The only person not safe around me is me."

"I've got about three minutes before they'll be getting themselves into trouble." Hopefully they'd be following last year's pattern and not the year before's. "Convince me."

"They," she watched him swallow hard. "They remind me too much of the past."

"This isn't Afghanistan, Evan."

"I understand that. This also isn't emergency leave from Afghanistan to arrive too late at my little sister's hospital bedside."

"Oh god, Evan, I didn't know. I'm so sorry," Krista hugged him despite the awkwardness of the heavy pack he still wore.

He remained stiff, burying his face against her shoulder for one long moment before standing back from her embrace.

"How did she die?" Krista barely managed a whisper.

Evan closed his eyes and faced off into the woods as if wishing he could transport himself somewhere…anywhere else. His voice when it finally came out was hoarse, dark.

"She went out into the woods and put .30-30 slug into her brain from my Winchester 94 deer rifle. She missed, partly. Some kids found her. I buried the damn gun with her; the only two things I ever loved." Then he opened his eyes and looked back at her, the pain pulled back behind a wall so deep that she couldn't believe he'd let her see behind it. "I think Mallory needs to talk to me. I can't leave until I know for sure that she's okay. I *have* to stay."

Krista didn't know what to do with such a good man. She could feel the heat of tears burning behind her eyes. She cried easily enough, usually from laughter at a good joke well played. This was different. His pain ripped at her gut. Unable to bear it, she pulled him into her arms again and held the injured boy who'd become a man. A man who would face his own deepest pain to help a girl he'd only met hours before.

In that moment, the world shifted beneath Krista's feet, the forest floor bucking and heaving against any hint of balance she'd previously known. She didn't know what the feeling was, but it rocked through her until there was no place in the world more steady than holding Evan Greene close.

Krista finally managed to step back, could hear the rising voices behind her that meant she needed to return soon, but couldn't quite make herself let go of him completely—unsure she'd be able to walk if she did. Afraid he might disappear like a wraith if she looked away for even a moment.

"Just give me a minute, Krista. Then I'll roll into camp just fine."

She nodded again, not trusting herself to speak. She kissed him hard. Not with the fire's heat that she'd been so looking forward to, but with everything her heart was feeling. He kissed her back then sent her on her way with a slap on the butt that was endearing rather than making her want to flatten him.

Krista waited until she was halfway around the curve, out of sight from both Evan and the campsite. There she stopped a moment to wipe at her eyes and have a good sniffle.

This better not be what she thought it was, but she more than half suspected she was head-over-heels gone on the quiet soldier. No time to think about it now. She wiped her eyes again to little effect.

Enough!

Happy face!

She slid her sunglasses into place and trotted around the curve and back into camp. The girls were just starting to mill around, wondering what to do next.

"Hey, now that's a great spot for a fire. Only one problem."

"What?" "C'mon, we did great, didn't we?"

"The problem," Krista announced over their complaints, "is that we have a great firepit…and no firewood. I think that it's time we learned what the axe side of your Pulaski is for. Let's go chop some wood."

As she got the girls organized to head into the woods, she glanced back at the trail. She was half afraid that Evan wouldn't be able to face his demons and might just have turned around and headed back to camp, or worse, be gone permanently before she returned.

Instead he stood there, once again at the threshold of shadow a single step from the sunny clearing. Thumbs hooked in pack straps, sunglasses in place, he looked every inch the amazing smokejumper, top soldier, and gorgeous man.

As she moved about the clearing, she could feel his eyes tracking her. And it was one of the best feelings of her life.

Chapter 8

It was evening and the last of the girls were out of the woods.

He did a running headcount that was so instinctive to his training that it wasn't conscious, it simply clicked over to "all accounted for" when the last girl had walked in with Krista. He noticed that the chaperones Mac and Zelda were lingering for a moment back in the shadows as a single outline.

Made him think of getting close to Krista, preferably when he wasn't on the verge of barfing up some memory.

She'd treated him okay despite his revelation. He'd never told that to anyone, not even his Green Beret buddies when he'd returned after a five-day emergency leave that had been two days of travel, one of visiting the morgue and dealing with Francine's possessions, and two of arrangements for a funeral only he attended. He hadn't told his parents when or where, because even if they were sober enough to hold their tongues they would have been unwilling to "be associated with such a thing." And he knew Francine wouldn't have wanted them there. They'd disowned him when he went military instead of some professorship, like it had served them so well.

They'd disowned Francine years before that.

If she had any friends, they hadn't surfaced.

The evning was a minute-to-minute battle; constant vigilance that he didn't let it overwhelm him again. The merry teasing of the girls made it easier. Mallory was joining in as well and Meaghan was staying close by her side.

But for that, Francine. If you'd had even one friend so staunch, maybe…

He shrugged it off for the hundredth time today.

Sorry, sis, he thought for perhaps the thousandth.

He'd been her only friend, her only shield. And he'd left.

"Are we really gonna eat these things?" Callie was holding up the plastic pouch of an MRE like it was a dead fish.

The sun had passed beyond the treetops and behind the massive peak of Mt. Hood. So even though it was still early in the evening, the clearing was heavily shadowed and the crackling fire offered more comfort than light.

"I was kinda hungry, but now…"

"Wimp!" Evan chided her. "What flavor did you get?"

"Damn straight I'm a wimp," she replied with a spunk that was easy to admire. "I got Southwest Beef and Black Beans. Why don't you go hunt us up some raw elk with your bare hands?"

"Hey, that's one of the better menus: spiced apple pieces, turkey nuggets. Yum!"

"You're weird," she wasn't buying it.

"Would you like some powdered hot chocolate with that?"

"Some what?" Callie looked at him cross-eyed.

"The Rook," Krista said as she poked at the fire a bit, "has this thing for hot chocolate mix, with the marshmallows."

More cries of "Wimp!" and "Aww, what a cute little boy!" sounded around the fire. It was music to his ears, because it meant he hadn't scared off the girls or slipped once again into some dark place without being aware of it.

Then he thought about it and got Mallory in his peripheral vision but kept talking to the effervescent Callie.

"No candy in that MRE menu, so you're safe."

Callie looked at him like he was completely brain dead.

"Seriously. Girls," he raised his voice and put on his command voice. "Do *not* eat the candy if your MRE has one. Seriously bad luck."

His tease got the expected round of disbelief and scoffing, then Evan lowered his voice.

"Superstition or not, there isn't a Special Forces soldier out in the field will eat the candy out of an MRE. They used to be in most of the twenty-four menus, but the Army figured it out eventually, only eight of them still have any."

He didn't often talk about what he'd been before. Like never.

Then he let his gaze focus on Mallory on the other side of the crackling fire. And he spoke to her while not appearing to stay focused on her.

"I spent six years in Afghanistan as a Special Forces Green Beret. I never ate a candy nor did any of the men in the ODA I commanded when they ultimately made me a captain. Five more years as a smokejumper, I still don't eat it."

They were all looking at him in some form of surprise. A soft buzz circled the fire quickly.

Krista was looking at him wide-eyed, whether at his past or that he'd revealed it, he couldn't tell.

At the moment he only cared about one girl's response. *I know things. I can help,* he'd practically shouted at Mallory.

Of the entire circle, she was the only one looking at him dead seriously. Slowly, as if it hurt her, she nodded once.

He returned the nod just enough for her alone to see, then turned back to the group.

"So seriously, don't be eating the candy. Though I can really recommend the powdered hot chocolate if you got a Mexican menu."

That got the laugh he was looking for.

# # #

Evan had his knife and his own MRE out, Pork Sausage with Cream Gravy. Crap! He thought they'd discontinued that one. Then he saw that it had last year's date on it. Well within the three-year shelf life, but ick! Powdered chocolate wasn't going to be any help here. Even doing a half swap with someone else for ingredients to add wouldn't make it more than barely palatable.

"Hang on a minute on those MREs," Krista called out.

He could see that Krista was listening for something. He knew her every movement well enough now that the slightest tilt of her head was a major giveaway.

He heard it before she did, but not by much; Krista was just that damned good in the woods.

Horse.

Horses.

Four or five by the sound of them. Coming toward the opposite side of the clearing from their own approach.

A string of horses wandered into camp. The first, a big tan gelding, was ridden by a long brunette in jeans and Western style shirt. She had a cowboy hat propped on her head. Behind her she led a string of horses.

"Hi, Laura," Krista called out. "Hey there, Mister Ed," she addressed the horse.

Evan waited half a moment to see if the horse answered and then shook his head to clear it.

Several of the girls scrambled to their feet and headed over to greet the horses.

Laura? This had to be Akbar's wife. The wilderness guide.

Damn, but they'd be an odd-looking couple. She was definitely taller and as slender as the lead smokejumper was broad shouldered. No way to see into anyone else's relationship.

Whatever she was like, he was willing to give her the benefit of the doubt if she'd brought real food.

"C'mon, Rook," Krista's voice called from somewhere among the milling women and horses. "Time to lend a hand. Last horse is yours."

Laura, astride the lead horse, warned him in a smooth voice, "Careful, Mister Ed isn't real partial to men."

"How did he take to Akbar?" Evan patted the horse's nose and only received a baleful look in return.

"Not well," she offered a merry giggle that didn't sound as silly on her as it should have.

He moved on down the line.

The second horse was carrying several large coolers. The one behind it had a heavy set of saddlebags filled with, he squeezed one, and guessed apples and oranges and other treats. The last horse, a beautiful gray mare who nuzzled his pocket—causing him to double back and steal an apple for her from the proceeding horse—was burdened with chainsaws, fuel, and rappelling equipment.

He laughed to himself. Krista was really running these girls through their paces. He unburdened the poor mare as fast as he could.

# # #

Krista woke the next morning to the bright roar of a chainsaw muffled by the surrounding trees.

She was terribly disoriented for a moment.

No matter where she turned, she couldn't see fire or smell smoke.

Nor could she see her lover. She'd been having this dream, of a handsome and naked Evan sleeping alongside her, his head on her shoulder, somehow convincing her she was beautiful and special. But the dream was fading rapidly and even the reality of Evan sleeping in just the next sleeping bag over was gone.

He wasn't there.

Two dozen empty sleeping bags were ranged around her.

Smokejumper camp.

Right.

She'd really been enjoying that dream, which must be the reason she hadn't heard Evan and the girls getting up.

Now she was blinking like an idiot in the post-dawn brightness.

Barely post-dawn.

Laura was gone, too.

But her horses were still tethered at the edge of the clearing.

Where were…her brain finally snapped to.

After feasting on hotdogs and hamburgers, potato chips and S'mores, their campfire had gone long into the night. They'd burned up the stock of wood except for one lone log, both ends rough-cut by high school girls wielding Pulaskis, that sat lonely by the blackened fire pit.

Her man was off with a chainsaw so that they could cook breakfast. It made her feel all warm and—

Then she heard the shift in tone. No longer just sawing away, it was the rapid shift back and forth of someone guiding a tree fall with the final angle of cut.

Krista scrabbled into her boots, stuffed the laces into the boot tops and sprinted off toward the sounds.

Just as she reached them, she saw it go.

The tree was a foot across, fifty feet high, gray and barkless with death. None of its branches bore the least sign of green, most of the small branches were gone. A long-dead snag that hadn't fallen.

It crackled and smashed through the higher branches of its neighbors and then, inexorably, accelerated until it crashed into the duff with a heavy boom that she could feel as much through her boot heels as her ears.

She'd arrived behind Evan, Laura had the girls standing well to the side of a fallen tree, at the safest angle and outside the possible fall zone. Each wore their hardhat and safety glasses.

And Evan stood close beside the trunk, holding the idling saw as it ticked over slowly. His pants were covered in sawdust, but in a tight t-shirt, he made an amazing picture. Manly man doing manly things; she could practically see the girls swooning.

Hell, she was practically swooning herself. How could the real man fully clothed be even more stunning than the naked one in her dream?

"Don't try this at home." He finally choked off the saw and the silence was deafening. "It takes a lot of practice to drop a simple tree like this one safely. One like that," he pointed with the blade of the saw up at a multiple snag—two leaners against a third, very old tree—"is called a widowmaker for a reason. I'd leave something like that piece of nasty to someone really skilled…like Krista." And he turned around to aim that radiant smile at her.

There was no way he could have heard her approach, but he knew she would be there. Had probably known that's where she'd end up before he even yanked the saw's starter cord.

The girls all looked at her in awe. The ones who'd been standing back at a safe distance moved closer, and the rest of them who'd rushed in from the campsite joined them.

Krista walked up beside Evan and barely resisted kissing the living daylights out of him right then and there. Instead she punched his arm hard enough to make him stagger—teach him to scare the crap out of her.

"Actually," she eyed the snag while the girls laughed, "on a fire, that snag is the kind of mess we hope burns up before we have to deal with it. That one is seriously dangerous. As a matter of fact, I don't want anyone walking over there. It may have been that way for weeks or years and it could stand another decade—or another minute. There's no way to tell."

"Well, we need some firewood if we want breakfast," Evan called out. "So, who wants to learn how to run a saw?"

Every hand in the group shot up.

He pointed his blade at Meaghan...rather than Mallory. Not what Krista had expected, but she was guessing that Evan probably knew best.

Some instinct had made Krista grab her hardhat and glasses, so she laced her boots and picked up the second saw that Evan had set off to the side. She waved Mallory forward and began using her as a live model for how to start and safely operate a saw.

Laura soon organized another group to split the cut sections into firewood with their Pulaskis—not the best log splitting tools, but they did the job easily enough on this old wood. It wasn't long before they had enough wood for a dozen campfires and it took multiple trips back to camp for everyone to transport the logs. As the last group headed off with heavy armloads, she snagged Evan.

She planned on kissing him for being so wonderful.

Instead, he grabbed her and shoved her back against a stout Doug fir on the side facing away from the girls. He drove against her: lips, hands, hips.

In seconds he had her moaning with a desperate need for more. She had a leg, then two around his hips to keep him close, her arms locked around his neck.

He kept her pinned against the rough bark, one hand scooped low to keep her from sliding downward, the other pressed so hard into her breast it would have hurt if it hadn't felt so incredibly good.

Some impossible eternity later, that was probably seconds but felt far longer, he backed off a half inch.

His breath was as short and ragged as hers and her heart hammered louder than a full-on wildfire.

"Good morning," his voice was hoarse with need. He nuzzled her lips a moment longer and then nipped her ever so lightly on the nose.

"Uh, hi!" she managed. "Can I ask a favor?"

"Name it," his dark eyes so close didn't let her think before she spoke.

"Can we arrange it so that you wake me up that way every morning?"

"What? A chainsaw 101 class?" Another kiss deep enough to keep her body humming.

"No," a breathy whisper—what was happening to her? "I mean this."

"Sure. Always glad to do whatever the Master Sergeant commands." Then he stroked his hands down her once, tracing every curve from neck to thigh and coaxing her to unlock her legs from around his waist.

She felt disconnected from her limbs, lightheaded and dizzy.

"Very glad to," he made it a final murmur against her lips. "Now I better make sure they know how to start a fire without burning down the forest." He headed back to camp whistling.

Krista laid back against the tree's bark—its roughness the only thing that kept her from sliding down onto the forest floor.

# # #

Evan knew nothing about the Oregon wilderness, except for the locales that had burned. The Zulies flew most of the West, covering Alaska to California from their Montana Base, but between the U.S. Forest Service smokejumpers in Redmond, Oregon and *the* elite contractor in the entire business—Mount Hood Aviation—there hadn't been much call for him to come to the state. At least not until he'd gotten a job here.

So, when Krista loaded them up with rappelling gear and bag lunches from Laura's stash, he shrugged and went along with the ride.

"When there's a crisis," Krista lectured as they trooped through the woods, "smokejumpers are first responders. On a wildfire, we're what's called a Type I Crew. In other words, the worse it is, the more likely they are to send us. But we can also be called out on flood relief, hurricanes, even oil spills."

"With my last outfit…" It still felt odd to refer to the Zulies in the past tense; he'd jumped with them for so long. "…I've done hiker search and rescue as well as jumping to downed aircraft that no one else can get to quickly."

"So, we need to know a lot about ropes and harnesses for safety work."

"Or if you get hung up in a tree while your jumping and need to lower yourself down."

That earned him a lot of surprised looks.

"Sure, jumping near a fire, the winds are incredibly unpredictable."

"As the Rook found out on his first fire with me," Krista teased him.

"I didn't land in a tree," he protested.

"No, he landed in the fire itself."

Which wasn't entirely accurate about the jump but was dead on when it came to Krista. He'd definitely landed in something wonderful and intense…and potentially incendiary if he didn't get her alone soon. So, he gave a "you caught me" shrug which had the girls laughing.

"We're going to teach you some basic rope work," Krista stopped at a long grassy slope. It was steep enough that it would be hard work to walk on, but if you fell you wouldn't roll very far.

They spent the rest of the morning with one end of the ropes tied off to a line of stout trees and the other through the brake on their rappelling harnesses. They got to the point where they were quite comfortable moving up and down the slope. Standing perpendicular to the slope they were steeply tipped from normal gravity, but they learned how to trust the equipment and work from those positions.

Thankfully it was a shadowed slope, because the rope practice was an intense workout and the sun was bright and warm. The girls would have cooked their brains if they did all this exercise in the sun.

Then after a lunch of MREs—which elicited all of the surprise and complaints he'd expected—Krista led them to a steep wall. The cliff wasn't vertical, but it would be a very hard wall to free climb and even harder to descend. It was less than a hundred feet, but to them it must have looked like a thousand.

Much to his surprise, after some initial hesitation, they all made their way down walking slowly backwards down the wall, practically lying flat in relation to gravity.

The excited cheering grew with each person who made it down until he was the only one left at the top of the ridge. He released and tossed each rope down except for one.

Over the very steepest section of the cliff, he doubled the last rope around a tree trunk rather than tying it off to one. He ran the two lines through the rings on his harness and knotted both ends so that he didn't rappel past the end of the ropes even though they were lying on the ground when he tossed them down.

"Clear below," he shouted down the cliff. They all backed away to the edges of the small clearing between the cliff base and the stream running down the valley; twenty faces staring up at him from beneath their hardhats.

Once he was sure they were clear, he did a Special Forces rappel. Kick hard off the cliff; let the rope fly. Cinch it to slow down just before swinging back to the cliff face. Time the next two-footed kick so that he didn't lose any momentum; let the rope fly again.

In seconds he was at the base of the cliff having only touched it three times, including the top. There was a stunned silence as he unknotted one of the ropes and tugged on the other until the free end of the line had passed around the tree at the top of the cliff and snaked down into a pile in the grass at his feet.

He finally heard a soft, "Holy shit!" from one of the girls. Neither of the chaperones made any attempt to hush her.

As he coiled the rope, he turned to face them. "That is a seriously advanced technique. Took me a long time to get it right with some of the best trainers in any military. But I just wanted to show you that there are whole different levels to each of these skills we're showing you."

"Right," Callie drawled it out. "Like they'd ever let a girl do that."

"Our senior pilot," Krista spoke up, "flew a Black Hawk helicopter with the Army's SOAR. They're the very best pilots; the same people who flew into bin Laden's compound. Annapolis, West Point, and the Air Force Academy are running fifteen to twenty percent women in every class now. Many Hotshot fire crews are a quarter women now. Smokies like me are still rare, but being a smokie is tough."

"There's a reason they call it the Special Forces of the fire-fighting," Evan acknowledged. "But we had three out of eighty in the Zulies." The look of determination that rippled through the group of girls was one of the best things he'd ever seen. The world had just opened for these young women. No small town would ever hold one of these back from anything she wanted to do.

He looked to Krista and knew this was the moment she'd been waiting for, this is why she had started this. Her face simply glowed with joy.

That.

That was what captivated him about her, the way her heart simply shone from her face.

He wondered at her strength that she'd found a way to climb to smokie on her own, and loved that she cared this deeply about helping others up by simply showing them what was possible.

"You want a model for all you can be?" He addressed the girls. Then he just pointed at Krista and all their faces turned to her.

She actually blushed and looked down, which was awfully cute on her.

And Evan wished he'd met more women like her over the years. Not just powerful in body and form, but independent and confident in who they were. Maybe meeting one was enough. Perhaps that was all any man was gifted, the chance to meet one woman who was so incredible.

He almost laughed. They'd humped each other's brains out only two or three times, managed to sleep together one single night, and fought a dozen different fires in three different states across four weeks, and here he was ready to sign up for a full-on relationship with her.

This isn't some Army enrollment, he warned himself. Though in retrospect he'd given that less thought at seventeen than he was giving Krista now at thirty-two. But it wasn't just some girlfriend or casual fuck either. He cared about her, deeply.

De oppresso liber indeed. The Green Berets read their Latin motto as "to free from oppression." But the actual translation was "from being an oppressed man, to being a free one."

Krista had broken with whatever her mysterious past was. These girls were breaking free even as he watched them.

He couldn't wish for anything greater for them.

Too bad he couldn't wish it for himself.

# # #

The afternoon passed in a blur.

Krista was still trying to adjust to how Evan saw her. It was no longer a surprise that a man as handsome as him found her physically attractive; he'd proven that beyond any possibility of doubt.

It was that he also saw her as…an ideal others could strive for? She'd never been a model for anything except how to be a royal pain in the ass to every smokie who slacked for even a second. Yet he had made the young women of Hood River High School look at her like she wasn't just someone special, she was also who they should try to be.

The girls had actually gotten a little shy around her, which she'd pretty much cleared up by nearly falling into the rushing river that was at the bottom of the valley they'd rappelled into. It wasn't that she was fooling around or being clumsy, it was just that she'd suddenly noticed that she and Evan were walking along the trail beside the river holding hands.

Right in front of everyone!

When had that happened?

And then she'd walked right off the edge of the trail and would have gone into the river if they *hadn't* been holding hands.

Once she recovered, she looked at him in some alarm. His smile was entirely too pleased with itself. She was half tempted to spin around and send him off into the river instead.

Two things stopped her.

One, it felt so damn good.

Two, the girls weren't reacting to it much at all. She didn't see coy whispers or sideways glances. Krista did notice several sighs as Evan made sure she was steady on her feet before they continued ahead.

She felt a sigh herself. She was good with ropes, but she'd never seen anything like the flying descent that Evan had done. While aided climbing and descending was a skill that smokies used, it was obviously one that Green Berets lived by. Knowledge of that hadn't made it one bit less dramatic. When he did that first kick and fall, her heart had choked her by the throat to think how much she could lose in that instant. Then he'd arrested, bounced off the cliff face with the perfect ease of a top-level hopscotch player working her way down a chalked sidewalk, and dropped another dozen meters.

And then he'd turned it around as a lesson to inspire young women...and now she was right back to where she'd started, with the day blurring behind her. The sole reality was Evan's hand anchoring her to the earth so that she didn't fly away.

They finally reached the ultimate destination she'd planned as a treat for the outing, the Tamanawas Falls. Forty feet wide, the hundred-foot falls hammered down into a rocky landing pool in a smooth curtain, throwing up a cloud of mist that softened and cooled the hot summer day. There was a big cave back behind the falls and soon the girls were off exploring.

Yet rather than joining them, she and Evan perched on a rock that offered a spectacular view, and also allowed them to keep an eye on the whole area.

"What's with…" she flexed her fingers in his but didn't let go.

He shrugged. "Seemed like a good idea at the time. I was standing there telling them all how wonderful you are, then it sunk in finally how wonderful you *are*."

"I don't know. Sounds like lust to me." Didn't sound anything *at all like lust*. Though she'd feel far more comfortable if it did.

"There's that, too," Evan agreed amiably.

She noticed that he was scanning the green bowl of the waterfall from behind his dark sunglasses, constantly on the lookout for the girls' safety; which was good because she couldn't focus for crap at the moment.

The area was thick with ferns and moss. The mist-slick, hard rock kept most of the trees small. It was a truly beautiful spot, one of her favorites in the entire National Forest. But she'd never been here with a man before. Not a man she was willing to hold hands with in public anyway. She tried to remember if there had ever been one of those before, but couldn't think of one.

"But there's also what you are doing for these girls," he continued in the same voice as if that didn't turn her world completely over.

In prior seasons, the smokies who'd helped out had gotten into the fun of it. Made sure the groups had a good and safe time. Without any prompting on her part, Evan had gone beyond and helped make it a life-changing event.

And based on how she was feeling, it wasn't only girls whose life was being changed. Even if he walked away tomorrow, he'd given her an image of herself that she'd never lose. She pounded it into her memory so that it would be anchored there for when this ended.

In this one instant she felt competent and desirable. She felt as if she'd actually become what she'd always strived to be and knew she could never be. Probably never would be again except for this moment.

Herself.

So she wrapped that up especially carefully and tucked it deep inside.

But there was even more.

She'd never given much thought about the man she'd want to be with for more than a fling. Most guys were just such… guys. Many of them good and decent, some total jerks, but all still just guys. She'd wanted something more, but had never been able to quantify what that meant.

More often than not Krista pictured herself as the rasty old smokejumper, maybe sent to the parachute loft after her knees gave out, smoking cigarettes (though she didn't smoke), and with a whiskey-rough voice (though she only drank the occasional beer). Her pastimes would be telling stories of "how it once was when there were *real* fires" and generally giving the rookies shit.

Now that Evan Greene sat beside her, still—unbelievably— holding her hand, she found it easy to quantify what she wanted in a man. There was the whole list sitting right beside her.

# # #

"Ready?" Evan checked Callie's harness. He'd already made sure she had on the heavily padded jumpsuit and that her helmet with the wire mesh face protection was securely in place.

"Ready," she acknowledged with the mix of fear and excitement that most of the girls had expressed the moment before the first jump.

Just like a spotter would, Evan leaned out the door and made sure the area was clear. Krista flagged him from the sawdust pit drop zone that she was ready.

He pulled his head back in, checked Callie once more through the mesh to make sure she wasn't hyperventilating, then slapped her on the shoulder and shouted, "Go! Go! Go!"

Without hesitation, Callie yanked herself out the door of the forty-foot jump tower. It was just a weather-weary platform with a safety railing on three sides. The fourth had a short wall with a jump door framed into it, so that it would feel more realistic.

She fell about ten feet before her harness yanked at her and stopped her fall like a dangling puppet. But the top of the harness was on a zip line that sent her shooting forward at about half of normal parachute landing speed so that there'd be almost no risk of injury.

He watched closely while listening to the delighted scream as she flew across the training area. With decent form, she hit feet first then tucked her arms in and let her momentum roll her onto her knee, hip, and—with a well-timed twist—onto her shoulder and back.

They'd spent an hour jumping off a block and into the sawdust pit practicing that landing. It wasn't something you learned immediately—it was unnatural to not fight the fall as you crashed into the ground, but most got it at least well enough that they weren't going to hurt themselves on the training setup.

Like so many of the others, Callie popped back to her feet and began dancing about as the adrenaline roared through her seeking some outlet.

He heard distant shouts of, "That totally rocked!" She wrapped Krista in a bear hug about her waist when Krista moved forward to free her from the harness. An embrace that left them both laughing.

It was the last afternoon of the camp and he was going to miss it. Yesterday they'd followed an easy, though somewhat longer, trail from the falls back to the campsite and had another nighttime campfire. The girls had been at ease, comfortable with him despite his being male. Krista had sat close, but they didn't make any "thing" of it and that had been good as well.

The hike back out this morning had been a merry affair despite the addition of empty coolers and a couple trash bags to their loads. He and Krista had toted out the saws, laying the blade on their shoulders and flopping a hand over the tip to balance the heavier engine dangling behind their shoulder. Laura had only brought out two small saws, so they hardly weighed anything. After their return to camp and another of Betsy's lunches, Krista had led them to jump training.

There'd been a fire call, but only about half the smokies had been needed. Most of the others were still sacked out or working over the gear, but Ant-man and Ox, who had been instructors in the prior years, came over to help out and cheer the girls on.

Still in the harness, Callie started an impromptu dance in the middle of the sawdust pit and the others began joining in.

Evan saw that they were missing one. Without even thinking about it, he knew who wasn't there; who hadn't jumped yet.

He turned and there, sitting in the far corner of the jump platform, was Mallory.

"I've been watching you."

"I might have noticed that," he admitted doing his best to sound casual. A quick glance revealed that Krista hadn't separated Callie and the harness yet.

"You always answer with truth when it matters."

Did he? "I'll try to cut down on that." But he knew he wouldn't. He also knew that was a dumb thing to say at the moment.

She waited with a maturity that wasn't supposed to happen to pretty eighteen-year-old girls. They weren't supposed to have things happen to them that forced them to grow up so fast. That was half the reason he'd gone to war in the first place, was to keep his sister from having to—*Shit!* He bit back against the pain.

"Sorry," he told her. "Bad joke. What's your question?"

"My brother was killed by a suicide bomber in Kabul. Did he die in vain?" Her voice was chill, emotionless. As flat and blunt as her question.

Evan wished he could see her better; she was hidden by all the jump gear that practically overwhelmed her slim body. The helmet wrapped around leaving only her face peeking out below the shadows cast by the raised mesh face screen.

He wished he could give her a hug and tell her a lie that somehow it would all be okay.

But even shadowed, her eyes said she knew better. That, Evan finally realized, was what made Mallory's beauty so shocking and so much richer than her classmates—those painfully aware, very adult eyes.

"I wish I could answer that," he scrubbed at his face seeking something wise to say. "All I know is that I stood beside some incredible soldiers and that we helped a lot of people. I honestly think they are better off for our having been there, but I don't know."

Her silence, her pain demanded truth—wise or not.

"I don't have any answers, Mallory. I swear to god that if I did, I'd give them to you. I wish I could answer why I survived six years in some other country's hell and my sister killed herself in Boise. I'd have given those answers to Francine if I had them. If I could bring her back for just ten seconds I'd tell her how god-awful sorry I am that I wasn't good enough to save her. Wasn't *there* enough to save her." He looked away and tried to pull himself together, tried to stop himself before he really began to scare the poor girl.

"Maybe," he managed a choking breath, "maybe your brother thought he was keeping you safe. Maybe he thought it was worth going there and risking himself for that. If I could have done that, saved Francine, I know that I would have thought it was worth any price. Including my life."

Mallory didn't say a word.

Evan stayed focused on Krista and when she signaled that the harness was clear, he pulled it back up the zip line using the thin tag line attached to the harness for that purpose.

Once he had it back up to the airplane "door," Mallory slipped forward and sat in the position safely inside the door where he'd attached the harness to nineteen other girls.

"You ready?" he kept his voice calm and professional.

She nodded.

Mallory didn't say a word as he buckled on the harness, double-checked the safety line that led up to a sliding metal loop on a second wire beside the zip line.

He went through the instructions by rote, making sure she acknowledged each step. It was as if he was putting both of them back together one strap, one buckle at a time—tying off their conversation so that they could both lock it safely away.

As he reached for her face mask, ready to seal off the last of it, she raised a hand to stop him. She looked up at him with tears in her eyes.

"I was so angry he left me. I couldn't even cry for him," she touched her hand to her wet cheeks and looked at them in surprise.

She brushed her fingertips and her tears on his cheek in a gentle gesture of thanks.

Then she moved forward into the door.

"Ready?" he asked. His tone neutral. His voice so rough it hurt.

"Ready," her voice was steady.

He stuck his head into the door frame and saw that the pit was clear and Krista was in position to help her land if there was a problem.

Instead of slapping her shoulder and yelling "Go! Go! Go!," he rested his hand on her shoulder and said, "You'll be great!"

She nodded and launched herself into space.

Mallory dropped down, slammed against the end of harness just like a real chute would grab at you when it opened, and then flew ahead. It felt as if she had left so many bad things behind.

Perhaps it was time he started doing the same.

# # #

Krista made sure that she was close, but Mallory landed clean. Actually almost perfectly, better than a smokie who'd had a season off and didn't have his jump legs back under him yet.

She didn't dance like Callie. Or scream or cheer. She simply flew. Mallory let Krista help her to her feet, but stripped the harness and the helmet herself.

Krista could see her tears that were more than the wind's passage but also the smile that hadn't shown much during the entire camp. Mallory simply stepped into her arms and held on tight. Krista hugged her back and looked up at the jump tower over Mallory's shoulder.

Evan sat there, legs dangling out the door, watching the two of them. She wished he was closer so that she could read his expression, but the tower was a hundred yards away and a dozen yards up.

Whatever Evan might be feeling, she knew she was looking at the best man she'd ever met.

And maybe, just maybe, Krista Thorson deserved such a man.

Chapter 9

Once the girls had a safety introduction by Denise the Firehawk mechanic and had their helicopter ride with Emily and Jeannie around the flanks of Mt. Hood, they climbed aboard their buses and were gone.

Watching twenty teenage girls group-hugging Evan had been a crackup.

Watching the gentle hug he'd given to Mallory had almost ripped out Krista's heart. Or perhaps it had healed it. She didn't even know anymore.

The camp felt unexpectedly quiet without them.

Krista went in search of Evan. Not in the showers, not in his bunk, not in the equipment sheds. She raided Betsy's kitchen for a couple of roast beef sandwiches and sodas, grabbed a pair of sleeping bags and headed out across the gravel parking lot.

She found him in the only logical place, sitting on "their" fallen Doug fir well into the woods, staring at the running stream.

Once again, she sat on the log close beside him.

She handed him a sandwich and a soda, "Thought we should get our calories first this time."

"Thanks." No smile, no tease, and no kiss. But if she was reading him right, also no dark-and-foul-mood either. He bit down on the sandwich and watched the forest.

"You were amazing with the girls, especially Mallory, but amazing with all of them." She wanted to ask what had happened between him and Mallory. What had they spoken of in that mere minute or two of privacy that had so changed the girl? Krista hadn't even seen the pain in her until Evan had somehow brushed it aside. But now it was as if something had been washed away and the true woman shone through.

"I'll be back for next season's tryouts," Mallory had informed her when they hugged goodbye. Krista just might have to talk to Akbar about considering letting a true rookie onto the team, for she had no question about Mallory's determination. She'd shifted from being driven away to being driven ahead. It was the same pain, just somehow…converted.

And most of all had been the look in her eye and the tone in her voice. Mallory had what it took to be a smokie.

Even trying to think about it made Krista's head hurt. She didn't have a lot of experience with those kinds of things. Though she suspected that Evan did and that's why his bouts of darkness had been so confusing to her.

Krista had a past that was both spectacularly good with her father and a major pain in the ass with school and men in general. Evan and Mallory had made trips to some other land she didn't begin to understand.

"Are you going to be explaining yourself anytime soon?" she asked before biting into her own tasteless sandwich.

"Huh?"

"Huh, he says. Yeah, that's a way to get between this girl's legs."

"Say what?" Finally, he turned to look at her. Then he looked down at his half eaten sandwich and back at her.

"Wow! Why am I thinking I just missed something really important?"

"Because you may be dense, but you aren't stupid, Rook. Which part of your brain am I talking to now?"

"I don't have multiple personality disorder," he bit down into the second half of his sandwich, but appeared to be aware of what he was doing for the first time.

"No? Let me count them for you. One, Special Forces Green Beret dude who can do some really amazing shit. Two, one of the best smokejumpers to ever join MHA. Three, Mr. Dark and Moody—who is very mystical and enticing, by the way. Kind of like a rattlesnake a person just can't seem to stop poking a stick at. Four, five, and six, a guy who can help a lost young woman find a center, utterly charm and inspire a whole troop of eighteen year old girls, and do the same to a twenty-eight year old one as well." She tapped her own chest and realized that "utterly charm" didn't begin to cover it.

"That's quite a list," he nodded as if they could all somehow be the same person. "Though I think most of that 'inspiring a whole troop' goes more to you than me. Anything else?"

"Seven, the best lover I've ever had."

"I admit," he finished his sandwich and reach for a soda. "I do like the sound of that last one. Would you like me to elaborate on that last attribute?"

"Soon, Rook, real soon."

She really wanted him to, but she had to make some sense of all of those conflicting men that were embodied in the man beside her.

"Tell me about your sister."

# # #

Evan had known that was coming, nodded that it was a fair question, but had to look away again. Had to turn away from Krista and look into a past far darker than the evening shadows around him. But, like the forest, there were also sun dapples of brightness in his memories that he'd forgotten—lost—until he spent three days with a group of young women with so much life in them.

"Twenty-eight. Francine would be your age if she'd lived, instead she was dead when she was the same age as Mallory. My kid sister, a total pain in the ass. Too damn smart, I guess, hell of a lot smarter than me anyway. She saw everything so clearly."

Evan looked out into the shadows beneath the trees but could see her fading memory no more clearly for all his searching.

"She saw people and would tell me about them." He could almost see Francine sitting by the stream giving him her *you doofus* look.

"I mean, she really saw them, in here," he thumped a hand against his chest. "The shit Mom and Dad pulled when we kids didn't meet their social agenda. It thought they were just weird. She's the one who pointed out they were near psychotic, alcoholic assholes who only cared about themselves. The girls and guys at school, the nasty ones with so little going for them that their egos were the only thing they could bring to the game."

Krista was holding his hand, but he couldn't turn to look at her.

"She was also naïve, a real sweet kid. Kept trying to help people. But if you want to help someone, you teach them how to be better at what they're good at. Green Berets taught me that. Francine kept pointing out what people were bad at, couldn't help herself any more than your poor stick-poked rattlesnake."

He took a deep breath, he had to finish the thought he'd spent a decade dodging. The forest was in the dead silence that came after the day-critters had roosted or burrowed, but the night ones hadn't yet come forth.

"I told Mallory that maybe I went Special Forces to defend my sister, and maybe that's why Mallory's brother went and died. To defend her."

Krista hissed in a sharp breath of sympathetic pain.

"I wish that really had been me. The truth is that I went in because I couldn't help Francine. No matter what I did, it just got worse. I should have gotten her a therapist, drugs, committed her under a suicide watch, something. But what did I know. I was going to be a soldier. That was my ticket out of our screwed up family and I took it."

The pain was too much, too deep, and the tears came though he fought against them; a battle he'd won for years now lost.

"Didn't know," he talked through the roughness in his throat, "that I was kicking out the last peg that was propping her up."

Krista folded him against her and he let her.

He'd thought by coming into the woods, he was buying time to get his act together after the crap he'd churned up inside himself while helping Mallory. So why had he come to the only special spot he and Krista had to call theirs if he was trying to avoid her?

She brushed her hands over him, kissed him atop the head as he lay against her, and murmured words he couldn't hear but could feel washing over him like the cool evening air.

The agony that had been burning in him was abating, retreating before Krista's instinctive acceptance and kindness, quenched against a past he couldn't fix. He'd been twenty-two, fresh out of college, and ready to take on the world. What did he know about pain yet? He could fix it for his sister, but maybe he could repay it in her name.

He pulled himself back from Krista. Pulled back until he could see her in the fading light of the sun gone behind Mount Hood, but not yet set.

"You do this next year, I'll be there. Don't care where I have to come from, even the goddamn grave. I'll be there. If I can save even one of them…" and his voice choked off, he couldn't continue.

# # #

Krista kissed him. What choice did she have?

She expected the attack, his need to purge the impossible pain he carried inside him. To lose himself in the act of sex. She would give that to him, whatever release he needed.

She half hoped for the tenderness that he'd so surprisingly given her the first time they'd made love. She wanted to try again to see what it felt like to be a woman who deserved tenderness.

She wasn't ready for the two combined.

With an intensity that had worried Akbar on the fire enough to come and ask her opinion before he spoke to Evan, her soldier boy turned his full focus on her.

Wordlessly, because he was clearly far beyond words, he focused completely on giving her exactly what she wanted. He didn't kiss her hard, but he did it so thoroughly that she felt as if she'd never truly been kissed before.

Evan unrolled one of the sleeping bags and eased her down onto it.

He didn't strip and take her, he didn't even pull off her shirt. Instead he used those big, powerful hands to stroke and mold her until she was no more than putty shaped to his pleasure.

When a fire burned, it could burn on the surface or climb up the ladder fuels—from brush to sapling to tree to the top where it formed a running crown fire that raced with the wind through the treetops independent of the fire below. Depending on the intensity of the fire, the forest's recovery might be fast or slow.

But sometimes it burned down instead of up.

A ground fire burned down into the deep duff or peat. Hard to detect and even harder to extinguish, it killed the very soil as it progressed. Soils could take decades to recover from an intense ground fire, the forest that would eventually return would have no hint of the old but had to be created anew.

That's the way Evan made love to her. Every move, every moment, he created such an intense heat, such an intense feeling that it burned away anything Krista had known about herself.

When he finally freed her from her clothes and she arched hard against his mouth and hands at the slightest touch, there was no room left for self doubt. There was no over-tall, big-boned, over-built smokejumper who happened to be female. All that remained behind was a woman helpless to do anything but respond to the man.

He entered her with the same gentle power, slow, tender, and wholly unstoppable. He rode her up until she knew only one thing. Until all else was erased.

Even as her body thrashed with the pleasure Evan sent scorching through her, Krista knew one clear, perfect truth.

With all his many facets, with his darkness and his passion and his joy, she was absolutely in love with him.

And that was something she wanted with no man.

# # #

Evan woke in the pre-dawn darkness to a hand stroking him.

Krista lay long and naked against him between the sleeping bags. The very first birds were singing in the trees. The brook was bubbling happily nearby.

"Wakey, wakey, Rook."

"How can you have your hand where you do and still call me that?" He rolled his hips to gain a little more pressure against her palm. "Not that I'm complaining about your hand's location."

"I didn't think you were," she murmured softly. She sheathed him and rose above him, sweeping the sleeping bag they'd been using as a blanket, like a cape to keep her warm against the cool morning air.

She settled down over him, a perfect fit. She started with a slow rock of her hips that had him closing his eyes to relish the feeling.

"Okay, as long as you do that," he managed to gasp out. "I don't mind if you insist on calling me Rook."

"Well," she did a side to side thing that she hadn't done before and he hoped that she did often in the future. "I can think of many things to call you, but I don't think you'd like them to be your tag among the crew."

"Understood. Let's keep those…oh my god, do that again… just between us."

"Look at me, Evan."

After a couple of failed attempts, he opened his eyes and did.

The breaking daylight was revealing Krista a little more each moment. He pulled her face down to kiss her good morning as she continued building the rhythm between them.

"Best sight I've ever woken to," he made a point of leering at her shadowed breasts. "Damn but you're an incredible woman, Krista."

"An incredibly large woman," there was a tone in her voice that rang false.

"Not filing any complaints," he tried a joke, but it didn't work.

She kept them moving, but the feeling had changed. The motion of their bodies was no longer he and Krista, it was just their bodies.

"Stop for a second. Just stop," he finally clamped his hands on her hips to hold her still.

She wouldn't look at him.

"Krista, now *you* need to look at *me*."

Only after several false attempts did she look at his eyes.

"I'm not the best guy around with words, but I know one thing for certain."

He waited until he got a soft, "What?"

"Any asshole that made you feel that you are one bit less than magnificent was an idiot. You are kind, big-hearted—"

"And I have big breasts that you are very partial to," she added with chagrin and no matching smile.

It was hard not to acknowledge where his hands had naturally drifted. "No arguments on that point. But if you think I'm with you because of your fine breasts, then you're even dumber than I am."

"So why are you with me?"

Evan tipped his head from one side to the other trying to figure out how to answer that. He was past wondering why he was having this conversation at this particular moment. "I've never been with a woman I wanted more or made me feel so crazy good. But that doesn't cover it."

"Then what does?"

"What is it with women needing words?"

"Because guys are incomprehensible and women get tired of always trying to explain them to ourselves."

Evan groaned in frustration and startled the same stupid squirrel watching them from atop the log.

What he wanted was to finish what they were well past halfway doing. Wiggling his hips didn't get him any response from the woman straddling him. She was warping his body with her amazing figure and his mind with her incredible eyes and impossible questions.

"Why am I with you?" he growled it out.

She nodded with the perfect complacency of someone who knew she was in absolute control. If only she'd looked happy about that power instead of so sad.

"Because there isn't another woman alive or dead I'd rather be with. When we have sex, I need you more afterward than I did before we started. I miss you every goddamn second we're apart. Not your body, you," he huffed out the last of it in total exasperation at his position. Here he was buried as deep as could be in an amazing woman kneeling over him so that her impossibly fit body was on incredible display…and he was being asked to think.

Krista was looking at him wide eyed.

"What?" he practically snapped at her.

In answer, she propped her hands on his chest, slowly closed her eyes, and tipped her head back as she shifted her hips in that amazing way she had earlier.

He wanted to demand an answer, but Krista didn't give him an opportunity. Instead she scooped a hand behind his neck and pulled him up to bury his face in her breasts.

Evan would worry about understanding women some other time.

# # #

Somehow he kept surprising her. Krista had no doubt that Evan enjoyed her body. Definitely a T-and-A man and heavy on the former. Her body sort of made sure most of her lovers were that way, though none had ever been as imaginative or thorough about it as Evan—as he was proving at this very moment sending convulsions of pleasure along her nerve endings.

But not a one of those past lovers, the good or the bad, had ever made a differentiation between her generous curves and the person who dwelled inside them.

Not a one until Evan.

She wasn't thanking him with her body. When his words sunk in, her body had simply decided that it desperately wanted what she'd so rudely interrupted with her questioning.

It was a final confirmation of something that had kept her awake for so long last night while Evan slept in her arms.

The whirlwind of sensations that shot through her came forth as a cry from both their throats.

For a moment, she gave herself completely to the wonder of the pounding that coursed through her system. That beat against the last doubts until her and Evan's bodies flagged and were still, though their breath continued to heave like they had just completed some harrowing parachute jump.

Last night she'd learned that she was completely gone on Evan; though she'd keep avoiding the "L" word, thank you very much. Crazy about him as she'd never been or even imagined being at any point in her life. And she…

An eerie sound built slowly in the breaking dawn light. At first she wondered if it was coming from Evan, then maybe from herself.

Finally the sound climbed high enough that she could identify the source as the MHA basecamp a few hundred yards away through the thick trees.

"Fire," she managed on a gasp.

Evan, his face still buried between her breasts, his arms locked around her back to keep her close, managed a nod. Then he offered a muffled, "Give me a second, just one goddamn second."

But the siren kept climbing until it echoed through the forest.

"Race you back to the camp," she managed on a gasp as she shoved down with her hips for one last glorious second.

His laugh, barely escaping between her breasts, was equally glorious.

Without question, the man who held her so close despite the siren, was just as gone on her as she was on him.

Of course, Evan probably didn't know that about himself yet. She'd make sure he got there. It would end, eventually; like all of her other relationships. But she was going to enjoy every last second of it.

Krista managed to reach her bra without displacing where he was buried up inside her. She had to push his face out of the way to slip it into place and tuck everything where it belonged.

"Spoilsport," he murmured reaching out and snagging both their t-shirts without moving from beneath her.

Less than sixty seconds after the alarm, they were racing back to the basecamp, and Krista didn't give a damn what any of her teammates thought about her disheveled state and the gorgeous man trying to catch up enough to grab her ass as they ran.

Chapter 10

Two hours later they were jumping a fire in the Bitterroot Mountains in Western Montana.

"I thought I was done with these damned mountains," Evan complained to Ox as they double-checked each other's gear before the jump. "This is Zulies territory."

"Yeah, I bet they're just having themselves nothing but fun up in the Alaska Range right at the moment; that Anchorage fire's a monster. Though I'm with you, bro. The Bitterroots suck."

They were as steep as the Hindu Kush, which meant missing a drop zone could land you in the next valley a several-hour hike away. Except the Bitterroots were covered with a towering conifer forest that was crackling dry with the heat and the drought that had been throttling the Northwest all year. Once on the ground, cutting a line across the steep terrain was a major fu—

"Dropping," Terry shouted and they all leaned to the windows to see just how ugly the streamers were this time.

Nothing unusual, the air currents were merely horrific—about standard for the Bitterroots.

He looked at Krista as she and Akbar prepared for their jump. Felt light-headed when he did. He'd always assumed that he'd never want to be with a woman long term. While he'd been in the military there was never any question of a woman waiting through a deployment, so he hadn't even tried for anything longer than a few nights. Once he'd gone civilian there'd been some nice ones, the type that might even last a season or two before fading away—if he'd given them the chance.

And there'd been the fine example of his parents, who had stayed together god alone knew why. Maybe they were compatibly nasty. It was all aimed at each other—he and Francine had just been sideline spectators to the main show—but that hadn't saved his sister.

Yet there was Krista, ducking into the door close behind Akbar. Even fully kitted up, between the powerful frame and enough curves to show through a thick jumpsuit, there was no question it was her. But there was the attitude as well.

The high-five that Evan now knew was going to cost Akbar another beer.

The way Krista kept an eye on "her charges" to make sure they were all ready for the jump. The way she cared so deeply about people just shone off her.

Mama Krista was the MHA Mama Bear…

That nickname wasn't going to stick either, but he could feel that he was getting closer.

He and Ox were second stick today, so Evan and Krista had sat close together for the flight. But old smokie habits took over and they were both asleep before the DC-3's wheels even lifted off the runway. Still, it had been nice to sleep even with just their shoulders leaning against each other.

He'd been the first to wake and had caught Akbar watching him closely. Krista had still been out, her head resting on his shoulder. Evan knew that Krista wasn't the only one to watch so closely over the team. But Akbar made no sign, positive or negative; he'd simply wait and see.

Now they were flying down and Evan scooted into the doorway position with Ox pressing close behind.

Like usual, Ox placed a knee in the middle of Evan's back, perfect position to shove him out before he was ready; though Ox never did, he certainly enjoyed his chosen role of harassing The Rook.

Evan did his final four-point check on the chute releases and cutaways, then he looked down at Akbar and Krista circling toward the drop zone.

The fire was only two dozen acres, but it had enough attitude that he wagered with himself that it would be a hundred before they could stop it.

Akbar and Krista fought the air currents that lashed them one way and the other. This time he'd have to call it a tie when they landed at opposite sides of the clearing; they now owed each other a beer.

He still had a moment before the plane was in final position for the second stick to jump, and he took it to enjoy the view. The Bitterroots might be hell to fight fire in, but it was also true wilderness that existed like few other places left in the States. He tried to think of someplace he'd rather be and couldn't.

He was three thousand feet above the most amazing woman he'd ever been with and they were going to fight a forest fire together. Life just didn't get much better.

Terry did his chatter-with-the-pilot thing until he was happy with the flight path. Then he pulled his head back inside and Evan changed his hands to the jump position.

"Ready?"

"Ready!"

Ready for what, was the question. His world had gotten a lot more interesting this summer than he'd ever counted on. He cared for the girls they'd taught at the camp and he cared for Krista more than should be possible. More than he was ready for? Maybe. He didn't know how to tell.

Terry's slap landed hard on his shoulder and he was out the door before the second "Go!" was out of Terry's mouth. The third one was lost behind him as Evan flew into the roar of the world's wind, ready for whatever came next.

When he dead-centered the landing he shouted to Akbar and Krista that they both owed him a beer.

Any response was muffled when Ox landed close behind him and his partner's collapsing parachute wholly enveloped Evan.

# # #

The blaze in the Bitterroots hit four hundred acres and took a week to kill.

The first bad injury of the season happened on that one, Jackal came down and planted one leg in a rabbit hole in the drop zone. He snapped his left tibia and tore his knee when his body tried to roll and his leg didn't follow. Axe had sat with him for the five cruel hours until a helicopter could reach them. Once they had the leg reset, he'd be in the parachute loft for the rest of the season repacking gear.

It was always a sobering moment, he could just as easily have broken his back or punched an artery and bled out before help could arrive.

But they did what smokies do, they beat down the blaze.

After the fire, Evan got one night with Krista—passed out wearing full gear in a helibase tent set up in a farmer's field. He figured it was a winner because at least they got real food at Betsy's roving chow tent when they woke up.

A brush fire in Mountain Home, Idaho took Evan a little too close to Boise for comfort—his parents still lived there, though his sister's ashes were buried in the River of No Return Wilderness along with all that had remained of his rifle after a long night in the heart of a campfire.

But before the Mountain Home blaze was fully contained, they were jumping another fire in Eastern Oregon.

"Having fun yet, Rook?" Krista shouted above the engine's roar as they were flying in.

Evan did his best to grin at her, but it was a pretty weary grin. "That last one was easier than teaching teenage girls. Have to see how this one is."

They jumped it. They beat it. Nick the Greek was favoring a shoulder after that and Ant-man did his best to stump along despite a sprained ankle. Smokies just weren't the sort of guys who quit while they could still walk—Ant-man strapped his ankle, popped a couple aspirin, and called it good.

They got a night in a cheap motel instead of a fire camp after that one, which everyone appreciated.

Evan scrubbed Krista down in the shower, and sent her off to bed while he finished himself because she was near to sliding down the drain herself. He knew she'd be asleep before he joined her, but it wasn't as if he had the energy for anything himself except to hold onto her and dream a bit.

He woke up sitting on the floor of the shower stall when the hot water ran out and he was forced to finish rinsing in ice water pumped directly off some glacier. Staggering to bed and reminding himself that it was all part of the joys of mid-season firefighting was usually sufficient. But, for the first time, he had a lady he was wanting some quality time with. Of course neither of them would give up a single fire to...

# # #

Krista jerked awake when the siren kicked off.

The clock said she'd had seven hours sleep.

The snores in the darkness told her that Evan probably had about the same. She remembered getting in the shower, and stubbing her toe as she stumbled back out, but not a whole lot else.

She lifted a hand to her face and sniffed tentatively under an arm. All she smelled was soap, thank god.

The siren was wrong; it was a fire truck siren, not a wildfire one.

She was almost back asleep when she heard Akbar's voice on a PA in the parking lot.

"Breakfast in five. Van to the airport in fifteen. Fire waiting."

That must have been a real popular move with the rest of the hotel's patrons—it was only five a.m.

Somehow Evan had slept through the siren.

There was a little light from the bathroom—apparently one of them had been too unconscious to turn out the light and had simply pulled the door mostly closed. Krista could just make out the man lying beside her.

Evan was face down on top of covers, with his pretty butt on display.

She smacked it hard.

"Ow! Hey! Wha...?" he managed in a running mumble.

"Wakey, wakey time, Rook. Fire's awaiting."

"Ha. Ha. Ha," he pulled the pillow over his head.

Krista went to smack that pretty butt again, but he must have felt her shift in weight through the mattress. He rolled and caught her hand. Leveraging her swing and his momentum he pulled her down on top of him.

But he'd misjudged and rolled them right off the edge of the bed.

Krista landed flat on her back with Evan crashing down atop her.

"Oof! You're heavy, Rook."

"That's not what you said last..." She could barely see him, they were on the side of the bed away from the bathroom, but she could feel his puzzlement. "...when was the last time we...?"

"Not right now, Rook. There's a fire. Other than the one I can feel growing against my body."

"You're joking?" he whined it like a little boy pleading to be spared.

"I thought macho Special Forces soldiers didn't whine." Just to torture them both a little, she grabbed his butt and pulled him against her for a long moment.

"Ex Special Forces. They threw me out."

"They what?" Krista froze. She couldn't imagine such a thing. It threatened to shatter her image of Evan Greene.

"Yeah. Happened right after I told them that six years, three tours, and five deployments was enough. They thought I was joking. I whined. On that basis alone, they decided that I wasn't their kind of guy."

Krista shoved him off her for being such a goof. She flicked on a bedside lamp so she could find her clothes.

He lay on the floor, half snarled up in the room's single wood-legged desk chair and making no real effort to untangle himself. "They tried bribing me for old times sake, gave me a rank bump and a Good Conduct medal for being a good boy. But I was too sneaky for them. I became a civilian instead," he winked at her.

"No you didn't, Rook," Krista clambered to her feet. Her clothes were strewn in a line from the front door to the bathroom, mixed in with Evan's. "You became a smokejumper." Each time she picked a piece of gear that was his, she tossed it across the room at him. He slowly disappeared under the growing pile of clothes landing atop him.

"Did I?" He still didn't get up from the floor. "Yeah, that sounds like the crazy ass sort of thing I'd do. Fire you say?"

"I'd be glad to send Akbar in to deliver a personal invite if you feel you need one."

"Bet you ten he'd make the invite with a fire hose," Evan whined in his best worried little boy voice.

Since she'd seen Akbar do that more than once to the other smokies, as well as dumping a bucket of water on Tim's head when he didn't wake up fast enough, she didn't take the bet.

"Besides," Evan clambered to his feet. "You're mostly dressed now. Where's the fun in that?"

Krista found Evan's underwear and heaved them at his face. Her beautiful lover, his naked body soft lit by the dim yellow bulb, started sorting through his clothes and pulling them on.

Whatever in the world she'd done right to wake with him beside her, she'd sure like to know so that she could keep doing it.

"I promise you fun later, Rook."

"Really?" he pretended to perk up.

"Sure," she promised him as she finished lacing her boots. "We're going to jump another fire, aren't we?"

He stuck his tongue out at her.

Krista grabbed him by his cotton long johns, reeking of firesmoke and sweat, and dragged him in close. "Fun. Later. Promise." Then, instead of kissing him, she shoved him sharply so that he tumbled back onto the bed. Before he could recover, she headed out the door to find some calories.

Besides, if she stayed even another second in that room, they were both going to miss the fire.

Chapter 11

*W*e're what?" *Krista's voice* squeaked and she went white.

Her skin and hair were so fair that she'd only lightly tanned despite making her living in the outdoors, but Evan was still impressed at the color change—and more than a little startled because nothing surprised Krista.

The van had rolled the sleep-fogged smokies back to the airport. Half of them, including himself, were still eating breakfast. Sausages hastily wrapped in a waffle, weird bacon-with-egg-and-turkey sandwiches, anything they'd been able to lay their hands on. Half gallon cartons of orange juice were being passed back and forth like moonshine jugs.

They were aloft while they were still eating, which was a challenge on a DC-3. The plane was a tail dragger which meant her aisle was steeply sloped because her butt normally sat on the ground, until she reached take-off speeds and then she climbed like a mother. The forces drove incautious smokies toward the tail of aircraft. This time most of them had their hands full of breakfast, so heavy boots were propped against others' hips or gear bags to keep from sliding to the stern in a confused heap.

They were aloft with the sunrise.

Once they had sorted themselves out and most of the eating was done, Akbar had told them where they were going.

And Krista had gone sheet white.

"We're what?" she repeated in a dead monotone, clutching Evan's upper arm with a desperation that was really starting to hurt despite the heavy jumpsuit.

"There's a fire," Akbar repeated himself, looking at her strangely. "On the Skagit River. Near a town named Concrete."

Krista looked like a beached fish, her jaw working but no sound making it out.

"What, do they have a big cement plant?" Evan went for a joke, hoping to elicit some response.

Her eyes simply went wider and she looked as if she was about to be ill. Then she began shaking her head slowly in denial. Thankfully she eased off on the vice grip around his bicep and dropped her hands lifelessly into her lap.

"Two plants, though I think they're both closed," Akbar said carefully. "Small town up in the northern Cascade Mountains."

"How bad?" Krista croaked out, clearly asking about the fire.

"It's—"

"Pretty bad," Evan cut off Akbar. "I'd say you're being a real mess at the moment. A pretty mess though."

Krista's glare did his heart good; it was a bit of the normal Krista showing through. Perhaps teasing her wasn't the best choice, but he had to snap her out of whatever was going on. She was worrying him.

He checked the rest of the guys. Most were finishing their night's sleep.

Only Ox had caught that something was going on and had managed to stay awake.

"It's not good," Akbar said gently. "Officially the Twin Sisters Fire, it started up on the Twin Sisters mountains from a runaway slash pile. Lumber company lit off a dozen piles of slash, one got away and they abandoned all the others. It lit a mile-wide front all at once. We have strong winds out of the northwest driving it toward the town of Concrete. They aren't evacuating the town yet, but they're watching it. What's the deal, Krista?"

"The deal?" Her voice was still sounded spaced out.

They'd jumped a half dozen fires already this year at least as bad.

Then Krista shook her head like a wet dog climbing out of a swamp.

"How soon do we get there?" And she rattled off a whole list of available asset questions without ever giving Akbar a chance to answer them.

"Krista," Evan finally shook her.

"What?" she snarled at him.

Thankfully it was Akbar who answered, "Explain what the hell is going on or you won't be jumping this one."

She stared blankly at Akbar for a long moment, then looked at Evan in deep distress. But he didn't know what was going on. So he did something they'd both been careful to never do in front of the crew. He took her hands, which were chilled and slick with panic sweat, and kissed her.

Ox grunted in surprise behind him. Evan ignored his jump partner. Time to deal with the fact that the Rookie was sleeping with Mama Krista later.

His kiss had the desired effect of surprising the daylights out of her and focusing her attention.

"Scaring us here, Krista. Just talk to me."

He saw slowly her coming back into her own. Her brilliant blue eyes which had been over-wide and distant, focused on his, then went watery with unshed tears. That unnerved him more than anything; he had no idea what to do if she actually cried.

When at last she spoke, it was barely a whisper. "We can't let those woods burn. Those are my woods."

"You grew up in Concrete?"

She nodded and bit her lower lip hard enough to drive the blood from it.

"Can you promise me you won't do anything stupid?"

She nodded, but he didn't quite trust it. And he wouldn't let anyone else take the risk if she did, but he knew to keep her off the fire would be a cruelty.

He looked over her shoulder at Akbar, "How would you and Ox like to buddy up on this one?"

Akbar the Great studied him carefully. He hadn't missed any of what had just happened, not even that Krista could well become a liability in the middle of the fire.

He started to shake his head, but Evan cut him off.

"I've got this one, Akbar. I'm good with it."

# # #

Krista had never felt so disoriented as the moment she eased up behind Evan in the DC-3's jump door.

Akbar and Ox were gone. She leaned out until she could see them fighting their way down through the air. Normally looking down was easy, Akbar might be powerfully built, but he was a shrimp. Evan was not. He sat tall in the door and the only reason she could see was that he was also leaning forward to watch the first stick's progress.

"Better than the Bitterroots, worse than Mountain Home," he shouted up at her encouragingly.

At least she liked to imagine that it was encouraging. No one had ever stood for her as Evan had…there'd never been a need for anyone to, but still it was surprising. Someone had her back. Not a soul had…not even her father really.

Focus, Krista. But all the commands in the world couldn't drag her eyes off the fire. Even as she watched, the blaze found a way past the Twin Sisters Divide at Bell Pass. To the west it was already past Lake Doreen and had begun torching along the South Fork Nooksack River, little more than a stream at this point.

The fire was spreading fast as it flowed into the valley, now moving on multiple fronts across two or three miles. And it moved like an arrow pointed at the town of Concrete, the Skagit River, and her entire childhood.

When she was twelve, she and her father had found a fallen madrona tree close by Lake Doreen—her father didn't harvest green trees for furniture, he let nature do the drying. The challenge was to find the wood in that narrow slot of time between dead and rotted, a very narrow window in the wet forests of the Pacific Northwest. They'd hauled the dense and heavy trunk the dozen miles back to his workshop over rough terrain and old fire service roads. Together they'd made a beautiful rocking chair that she'd lusted after madly long before they were done with the making of it.

Despite their desperate situation and the high price the rocker would have brought, he insisted that it was her thirteenth birthday present, as she was a young woman now she deserved something fine. It was one of the few possessions left of her childhood and it dominated her tiny private room back in the MHA barracks. Grandpop's knife even now on her hip, that chair, and Pop's old Ford pickup—which would be a classic now…if she ever got around to restoring it—were all she had left other than memories and a few photos.

Terry's slap came on her jump partner's shoulder and he was gone from in front of her.

Krista looked at Terry who stared up at her in shock.

"Go!" he shouted in urgent surprise and reflex jerked her out the door.

She was much farther behind Akbar than normal.

Except it wasn't Akbar

It was Evan.

Despite the distance between them and the heavy masks they both wore, she could feel his dark gaze boring into her.

He pulled his chute.

Her count!

He'd been waiting to make sure she was counting—and she wasn't.

Nor had she done the 360-degree survey to make sure she was in the clear. She did a quick safety check as she continued to fall. She was nearly on top of Evan's position before she pulled her own ripcord.

The chute jerked her hard—crotch and breasts; she should have cinched the thigh and chest bands more tightly.

But she'd forgotten.

Now she was too low, exactly the same height as Evan rather than safely above him. She tried to adjust her rate of descent, but that's when the first fire-hot gust slapped at her and sent her sailing in a direction she didn't want to go. In this turbulence, slowing her descent would also risk collapsing her chute.

So, they spun and dodged about each other for the last thousand feet into the drop zone. They both managed to avoid the trees, but only because Evan was kind enough to land on a small open spot on the far side of Bell Creek. He had to wade back across it and took a fair amount of teasing for his "missed landing" from the other smokies.

"Left-Bank Rook," almost stuck when Nick the Greek shouted it out. But Krista didn't pick it up, still it was a close call, him being tagged with that for his entire career with MHA.

She felt awful, but when she tried to apologize, he shut her down.

"You stick close by me," he whispered fast and quiet while the last stick was landing. "Don't do anything stupid and we don't have a problem. Roger that?"

"Roger that," she agreed hastily. She'd never needed someone to watch her back. It was an uncomfortable sensation—

shrugging her shoulders didn't shake it off—that this time she just might need the help.

When their paracargo gear also landed across the stream, much of it in the trees, Evan got his payback. All of the smokejumpers had to slosh back and forth several times through the ice-cold, thigh-deep water that poured off the glaciers of Mt. Baker before everything was consolidated in one spot.

Chapter 12

*T*he fire had the dry forest in its sights and it seemed that no matter what they did, it wasn't going down.

Evan had led the strike team of Krista, Nick, Ant-man, Axe, and Riverboat two thousand feet up the side of the South Fork Divide. They created a firebreak line the whole way up in order to narrow and focus the fire toward where he knew the battle would be.

Akbar, Ox, and the rest of the first plane load were headed down the valley of the South Fork Nooksack River. It would be a far more difficult target to secure. When the second load of smokies jumped, they'd probably all go to help Akbar.

He'd wished he'd watched the fire more during his jump, but when Krista hadn't jumped, then followed him late, he'd spent all his attention willing her to pull her ripcord. At any altitude, he didn't care. *Just pull the damned thing!* he'd finally shouted and she finally did, though there was no way she could have heard him.

He'd been on the verge of shutting his eyes so he didn't have to watch the most amazing woman he'd ever met do a "chute failed to open"—because she was too scattered to pull the cord. Worse, he'd been the one to let her jump, so he'd have been the one who'd killed her. He'd cried out in relief when she finally yanked the rip cord. Evan was so happy when she made it down in good form that he'd been ready to forgive anything, even freezing his nuts off when he waded that bitterly cold creek.

He pulled Nick the Greek aside and told him to keep a sharp eye on Krista and then placed her on the line between Nick and himself. Evan needn't have worried.

On the line, Krista was head down. Rather than doing her normal work of any two other smokejumpers, she was doing more like four or five.

Evan had to struggle to keep up.

As a result, their team moved at manic speeds, climbing and cutting, bucking tree trunks into sections, and swamping branches downwind of the growing firebreak.

They cut soil deep and scraped it hard, often down to bare rock because the steep slopes held little soil. Their Pulaskis were a blur of sharp steel and more than once he had to tell Krista to ease up because a poorly swung Pulaski could cut through her boot leather and flesh far more easily than the root-entwined sod they were hacking at.

Five hours since the jump, he had Ant-man run the line to make sure everyone was staying hydrated and taking a break for an energy bar. He wanted to do it himself, but he didn't dare leave Krista.

"Drink, Krista."

She ignored him.

"Krista Thorson…"

"Out of my way, Rook."

On her next upstroke with the axe, he grabbed the handle.

She was so powerful, she almost tumbled him over with her attempted downstroke.

But he braced and held on.

"Fine," she let go abruptly and he actually did fall over backwards at the sudden release of the tool.

"You just gonna lie there, Rook?" She knocked back the contents of her water bottle and looked down at him. "We do have a fire to fight you know."

When she grabbed for her Pulaski he pulled it away even though he was still on his butt.

"Okay, Mom," she snarled, but took out a couple of Snickers and began wolfing them down.

He climbed back to his feet. Before returning her Pulaski, he kissed her on the nose while she chewed. "Good girl."

"Go jump in a hot spot, Rook."

"Yes, ma'am," he saluted.

When she fisted him in the ribs, none too gently, he felt much better about her mental state.

In moments they were both back at it. It was obvious that she was taking this fire personally. She'd gone to some dark place where this was a contest of wills, never a good bet against a wildfire.

Evan had once watched an eight-year Zulie snap, right out on the fireline. They'd been working it steadily for four days with only a couple of short breaks; the whole team riding the edge of hallucinations caused by lack of sleep. The Zulie had started yelling at the fire. Not the normal trash-talking a smokie sometimes did to the flames about its mother and the ember it rode in on, but a screaming rant. It had taken five guys to drag him off the line and back to safety when he strode up to "get in the fire's face." Suddenly calm, a helo had medevaced him out strapped to a stretcher. He was gone; never came back. Last word said he was teaching high school English in Missouri.

Evan would be damned if he was going to lose Krista to the fire, but he didn't know what to do other than fight it alongside her.

They were both swamping for Nick and Ant-man who were on the saws when Krista croaked at him from a voice gone hoarse with smoke and lack of use.

"Blowup."

He stopped to listen.

Blowups typically happened between two and four in the afternoon. When the day was at its hottest and the last tiny bits of moisture were sucked out of the trees. The intense dryness in his throat told him they were under ten percent humidity. There was a tipping point between desperately dry forest and tinder dry—the latter needing only the tiniest encouragement to explode into flame.

Then he felt it. The wind shift.

In one way, it was incredibly encouraging. Whatever headspace his gal was in, her fire senses—which were the best he'd ever seen—were fully engaged and she was listening to them.

The wind shift was alwayss one of the scariest and least predictable moments on a wildfire.

The world's winds had been driving the fire steadily toward their position, down out of Bell Pass across Bell Creek, and climbing the ridge of the South Fork Divide.

The burn now covered much of the wide valley between Twin Sisters Divide and their position. They had come up Bell Creek to the east side of Loomis Mountain and Akbar's team had followed the South Fork Nooksack River to the western saddle between the Twin Sister's ridge and Loomis.

The air was impossibly still, despite the roaring of the chainsaws and the grunts of the laboring crew. All sounds fell on dead air and were oddly muffled. One by one the other smokies stopped what they were doing and looked up from their tasks.

Even the heavy pounding of the big Firehawk helicopters, passing close by overhead as they delivered thousand-gallon loads of retardant to the unburned forest behind the fireline, seemed to slow. It was like that slo-mo moment in war movies before everything went to shit.

Which, Evan knew, was exactly what was about to happen.

"Cone of silence," he agreed with Krista. He hated this moment. The heat of the sun pounding against his Nomex and not the least breath of a breeze to cool him. His hardhat, no longer protection but now a baking oven threatening to cook his brain. His gloves stuck to him by his own sweat.

Then the wind returned, in the opposite direction to how it had been blowing steadily all morning, feeding their faces with smoke.

Now he tasted fresh, clear air for the first time since they'd jumped this morning.

As gently as a whisper, it turned and began blowing toward the still distant fire. The wildfire would grow two or three times in ferocity and height in the next ten minutes as it sucked oxygen in from every direction.

Even as he listened, the thick sap in the giant Douglas fir trees down in the valley began cooking off. With that harsh body-pounding thump of 155mm M777 howitzer shells, trees exploded in the suddenly increased heat.

"Light the backfire now," he and Krista screamed out in unison, breaking their mutual paralysis. They laughed at the exact synchronicity of their calls even as they rushed across the fireline and grabbed up drip torches.

The cans of gas-diesel mix had a spout that dribbled out over a flaming wick. In moments, they were both splashing fire along the entire fireline, on the wildfire's side of the break.

The growing wind, driving toward the heart of the fire, whipped their tiny fires to life. Little splashes of fuel turned dry grass into flaming torches. That in turn lit the lower branches of the nearby trees.

The wind had already built to ten miles an hour and was growing quickly.

He and Krista turned in opposite directions and they sprinted down the line dribbling their bits of fire.

Mark Henderson up in the Incident Commander's plane had reacted before Evan had time to even think to call him. Suddenly a line of helos were pounding the fireline close behind him with heavy retardant loads.

As usual, the fire had chosen the when and the where of the next battle.

Thick showers of gooey red slammed into the forest coating branches with a slime that would block oxygen from reaching the wood. A hot ember cast into that would die—the wood was dry enough to burn and the embers would be hot enough, but with no oxygen, there was no fire.

The wind now roared down the slope from all directions to feed the blowup of the wildfire. North, east, south, and west— all winds blew toward the center and the fire erupted.

Orange flames, bright with heat and dark with ash, shot five hundred feet into the sky. Hundred foot trees were uprooted and tossed aloft like blades of straw. The roar was so loud that Evan couldn't hear even his own shout of wonder.

Each time he saw this, it was new. And rarely had he seen it so clearly. It lay spread out like a textbook drawing across the valley to his perfect seat atop the ridge. This was nature at her most primal, most dangerous, and most dramatic.

It was out of their hands now.

The backfire was ripped downhill toward the mighty blaze, adding its heat to the raging main fire sending it even higher and hotter. But what the backfire had also done, despite being a lower intensity burn, was consume much of the fuel that covered the face of the ridge below their fireline.

Krista came to stand beside him in the impossible silence of the pause between preparation and battle.

For a moment they leaned their shoulders together. The spectacle was awe-inspiring, and for the first time he was with someone who fully shared that awe.

Girls from bars would always ask, "You jump out of planes?" or "Isn't it dangerous?"

He'd get so tired of explaining the basics that sometimes it wasn't even worth the effort to pick up a woman.

He had none of that with Krista. They shared a passion, a language…and a need. It wasn't just a need for sex, it was fast becoming a need for her. He'd been thinking about that a lot while working the fire—ever since that terrifying moment when he thought she wasn't going to pull the chute.

He turned from the fire to watch her profile. Her smoke-smeared face looked pale from the effort she'd been expending; his probably looked little better. She was focused, concentrating on the blowup. But clearly aware of his inspection, a smile touched her lips.

Gods but this woman made him feel good.

The only problem was that the Evan Greene he knew never needed anyone. And the one person who'd needed him, he'd let down in the worst way possible.

The other smokies of their team gathered along the top of the ridge while they watched the smoke climb like an atom bomb. A great column of fire and smoke and heat soared aloft so fast that it shattered against the denser air above and formed a mushroom cloud.

Somewhere far aloft, the cloud of smoke—nearly white because it had dropped most of its ash after its initial meteoric rise—hit the jet stream and was sheared off and smeared eastward.

Still unable to speak over the roar of the fire, Evan dispersed them back to the line with hand signals. The second part of the battle was about to begin.

# # #

Krista still couldn't believe that they'd fought the fire to a standstill.

What flames did try to crest the ridge, were low, weakened by the loss of fuel burned in the backfire. They were still twenty and thirty feet of hell when they hit the fireline, but that was better than two hundred.

When embers sparked over the line, they either died in the retardant or were beaten down by the smokies before they could spread. During the daylight hours, they often called up one of MHA's smaller helos to douse a particularly stubborn spot fire.

It was well past dark when they finally had it contained, but the fire was blocked. This fire at least would never cross over the South Fork Divide.

By midnight, it was beaten and the sky began to clear as the smoke cooled and dissipated. The moon finally had a location, a bright spot beyond the smoke, even if there were no clear views of the sky yet.

Krista stood on a smooth area of exposed bedrock, black ash surrounded her in every direction.

A man moved toward her through the falling darkness, lit by the dying flames, a bright headlamp shining ahead of him. She couldn't see his face.

But no other man moved like that and Krista would know Evan Greene anywhere.

"Hey there, Rook."

"Hey, Pretty Lady."

She managed not to snort in derision. If he wanted to see her that way, she wasn't going to complain even if she didn't believe him.

He moseyed to a stop in front of her and killed his headlamp. "Fought your first fire to a standstill."

"You mean we killed its ass. And this isn't my first dance."

"You dance, Rook?" She loved that Evan shifted her statement to include the team though it had been just a tease. *We* even though he'd led the fight the whole way and everyone knew it. He'd handled her panicked efforts to save the forest of her youth right in stride without so much as blinking.

"Find me the right lady, I'll dance all night," he moved in close, rested one hand on her utility belt and wrapped the other around her hand on her Pulaski's handle. He pulled her in and began rocking them back and forth on the small patch of rock.

"I'll take you up on that one, Rook," she leaned in, not caring that he smelled of firesmoke.

"Still gonna stick me with that tag?"

"Until I got better, yep! You're stuck with it."

He harrumphed, but held her a little tighter. She went to lean her head on his shoulder in a totally mushy move that she'd never really understood when she'd seen other women do it. The fact that her hardhat ended up klonking against Evan's only made the moment more uniquely theirs.

Then he stopped as if quick frozen in place. His grip hardened against her.

Krista turned to follow his gaze, forcing her hand free from his clenched grasp so that she could turn to look.

Due south, beyond the crest of Loomis Mountain, there was an orange glow filling the sky.

Their fireline had held.

Akbar's hadn't.

The valley of the South Fork Nooksack was burning—funneling its fire straight down to the Skagit River.

Chapter 13

Emily Beale was still aloft in her Firehawk when he called, which Evan took to be a bad sign. The helos usually bedded down from sunset to sunrise. Night flying took special skills, which MHA's senior pilot definitely possessed, and also earned special bonuses. The U.S. Forest Service Incident Commander had to authorize the budget for night flights and they didn't do that very often.

A little quick wrangling and he had Emily on her way to pick them up after she was done moving Akbar's team down the valley. Krista was hustling about, getting the other smokies to gather their gear while Evan ran a chainsaw and cleared a helispot.

Starting from Krista's small dance floor, he circled out fifty feet in all directions and cut down any remaining trees or stumps that stuck up more than three feet high. The helo itself needed a spot ten-by-forty feet cleared to land in, but the spinning rotor blades needed a sixty-foot diameter circle with nothing sticking up high enough to snag a blade—which meant they had to clear a hundred feet for safety.

He finished the same time they did. Smokies left nothing behind, not a hose, not a parachute, not a piece of trash. They were there to defend the forests, not screw them up like so many did.

Evan tried to remind himself of that as he clambered up and down over the heavy slash he'd created, nicking off the occasional branch that stuck upward from the felled trees as he went. Most of the branches had been burned away, so that didn't take long.

# # #

While they waited for Emily to arrive they ate, but didn't talk much. It was past midnight and they had pushed hard since early morning. But for a smokie as skilled as Akbar to have lost the line he'd chosen meant that it must have been grim and he'd need help badly.

Krista felt hammered, both physically and emotionally. She'd been holding on so tightly.

In one direction, she could look at all they'd accomplished. The bulk of the valley defined by Bell Creek still burned, but they'd contained it. Now it would be up to the ground crews, who'd only recently arrived at the base of the fire, to kill it the rest of the way. The area would need a major recovery team after that, this forest had been burned hard and wouldn't be springing back easily.

It was the other direction that was making the smokies silent rather than victorious.

To the south, the orange glow was climbing. They were below the peak of Loomis Mountain, so the rocky peak was outlined in an arc of smoke glowing deep and dangerous orange. The stars which had finally begun showing to the east were blanketed out by the smoke still rising heavily from the west. Even though they sat in silence, the clear air was a relief after eighteen hours of eating smoke.

Krista felt her throat choke closed.

Hearty Creek and all of the animal habitats there, burned. George Peterson Butte, one of the best viewpoints west of the South Fork Nooksack, probably now a pillar of fire.

"C'mon!" she growled at the night because sitting still was killing her.

No one responded.

They couldn't know.

To them it was just another fire.

The Twin Sisters Fire was erasing her past. One burning acre after another, it was killing off and erasing everything she'd known as if it had never been. Didn't anyone understand how little she had to spare?

A hand slid out of the darkness and rested on her shoulder. "Easy, Krista. We'll stop it. The forest will come back."

"But it won't be the same."

Evan rubbed her shoulder in what he surely thought was a comforting way.

And it was comforting, damn him. She wanted something to rail against and he wasn't giving her a target.

"The past is never the same," he whispered and she could hear his pain.

Yet another thing they had in common, though she had no way to speak of it.

And how could she help but be in love with a man who reached out from inside his own pain to comfort her.

# # #

"Glad you're still flying," Evan shouted to Emily as he slid aboard the helo and leaned forward in the gap between the pilots' seats. "Saving a tired crew from a tough hike."

MHA's lead pilot looked back grimly, "It's what I live for."

Emily Beale was rock steady. Never happy-go-lucky, but never down either. She was the solid bastion that held MHA's pilots to such incredible standards. For her to be grim…

"How bad?" he asked.

"Akbar lost half of his gear. He had six people ride out the blowup under their foil fire shelters on a rocky island in the middle of the river. Jeannie had to medevac two to the hospital for second degree burns. Prognosis is good on them, only burned on the extremities."

"Shit!" was all he could think to say as the smokies piled gear in behind him. Deploying shelters was a last ditch solution, only used when every pre-planned escape route had failed.

"That's why I'm still aloft, running him fresh supplies because it's too dark to safely drop any paracargo and he can't wait until morning."

Evan tried to remember his map, "Where's he setting up?"

"Goat Mountain."

"Whoa!" That he remembered clearly enough, too clearly.

It had the advantage of being far from the present fire, but it would be a last ditch battle before the town. If the fire crossed over or found a way around the forty-seven hundred foot peak, it would sweep down the brutal valleys and near vertical cliffs of the southern face in less than an hour—far too little time to build another defensive line.

If it did escape them it would scorch Krista's home town of Concrete right off the map, jump the Skagit River, and race off into the Mt. Baker-Snoqualmie National Forest without blinking.

He remembered how it felt flying in with his ODA attacking an objective up in Lataband Pass, knowing that a lot of munitions supplies were going to reach the bad guys if they didn't stop them that night. And that would mean a lot of dead soldiers over the next months.

"Not gonna happen!" Evan yelled back at the fire crew.

"Right, Rook!" "You bet!" He could tell they were behind him even though they had no idea what was lying in wait for them.

"This town is *not* gonna burn!"

The shouted agreement sounded with a renewed energy.

Krista looked up at him as they sat on the hard decking of the helo's cargo bay.

"We won't let it happen," he said to her as softly as the rotors.

She nodded, uncertainly, then with more confidence, and finally with conviction.

Evan turned to watch out the front window as they climbed into the night sky. Six of them and their mound of gear barely fit into the Firehawk's big cargo bay. Within moments, the smokies had located a couple of fatboy boxes stowed aboard the helo and broken them open to restock their PG bags. Someone shoved a banana into his hand. To make it easier to peel, he bit into the stem—tasting that sharp bitterness and not caring.

When they flew clear of the top of Loomis Mountain, the bitterness didn't stop, even though he was now down to the sweetly ripe fruit.

Akbar's original fireline had been a wide slice between George Peterson Butte and Loomis Mountain. The two-mile wide valley carved by the South Fork Nooksack had clearly served as a funnel when blowup occurred. On this, the west side of Loomis Mountain, it had blown down the valley like a howitzer.

The fireline had never stood a chance no matter how deeply it was cut.

Now spread below them was a towering wildfire. With sunset, the winds had died and the humidity had climbed a few points. That wasn't stopping this fire, it was too big, too dug in, but the change was slowing the it down.

Right now it was two miles wide and a half dozen long, coming up fast on ten thousand acres. If it wasn't quite that big yet, it certainly would be by morning. And it would be climbing Goat Mountain by nightfall. They had half a night and a day to stop it.

"Not much sleeping in tonight," Krista whispered beside him.

"Not much."

# # #

From her perch on Goat Mountain, Krista watched as landmark after landmark was eaten during the long day. There went the old oak she and Pop camped beneath so many times and the spot she'd bagged her first deer with her bow and known that she was the one making sure they hadn't gone hungry that month.

The fire was hot enough to send most of the smoke upward. That was a good thing, because it saved them from breathing smoke all day. It also totally sucked because she could watch her childhood being erased with each passing hour.

By the time blowup hit on that second afternoon of the fire, Akbar had a line all down the south and west side of the fire. The helos and four large airtankers had inundated the forest beyond the line with long stripes of red retardant. The backfire wasn't as effective as the one the day before above the South Fork Divide, but it did the job.

The fire was narrowed and turned.

And the flames was mighty pissed about it.

"Works for me," she told it. She was pretty damn pissed too.

Goat Mountain was going to be hammered, but Akbar had made a good call, they were ready for it. Or as ready as they could be.

So, in between felling trees, swamping branches, and sweating like a pig in the midday heat, she watched the fire creep toward them.

There went the Jefferson's couch, a beautiful spruce she and Pop had found lying in the deep shade along Wanlick Creek.

The cedar for the Michelson's dining room set had fallen at Springsteen Lake on of the best swimming spots she'd ever found. When it took out the aspen that one long-ago autumn was, "Spilling gold coins all over us, Krissy," she knew her father was truly dead and gone. Then the white oak…

Krista turned her back on the fire and did her best to not look again.

Chapter 14

Evan had fought across the sands of Afghanistan.
He'd jumped two-hundred-and-twenty-three fires over the last five years.

He'd been in his fair share of bar brawls.

This was about the ugliest and most impressive battle he'd ever seen.

They had joined up with Akbar's crew at two a.m. A fire normally called for two to six smokejumpers. A bad one was jumped by a dozen. The Bell Creek Fire threatening Concrete and the Skagit Valley had the entire MHA contingent of twenty-four smokies and a half-dozen Zulies who'd been returning from Alaska and gotten rerouted.

The fire reached Goat Mountain at sunset. The sky was a fantastic blood red painted in grand swirls by the ash and smoke.

Aircraft had been circling above them all day. Mount Hood Aviation had all six of their helicopters ducking in and out a hundred feet above the treetops, ranging from the thousand-gallon powerhouse of the Firehawks to the little MD500 spot fire killers.

The Forest Service had two of the new, jet-powered BAe-146 fixed-wing air tankers dumping three-thousand gallon loads of retardant in long red stripes. They scattered the crowd of helos with their long straight runs at equally low altitudes.

Circling above them all was MHA's Incident Commander Air Mark Henderson in his Beech King Air.

Even in pitched battle while in Special Forces, Evan had never seen such an array of air support all in the same place.

A red biplane buzzed around the edge of the fire. Moving through the sunset-and-fire-hazed smoke like it was dodging about a World War I battlefield.

"What the hell?"

"What day is it?" Krista asked beside him. "Friday?"

"Thursday, I think." Evan watched as one of the helos raced over toward it. Despite the distance, he could hear snatches of someone yelling at the biplane pilot over a PA. Airspace above wildfires was always closed to all other air traffic for safety reasons.

The biplane did a wingover and dove away, back toward the Skagit River.

"Early arrival. Friday through Sunday there's the North Cascades Vintage Fly-In. It's one of the big annual events for Concrete. Good thing the helos are based out of Skagit Regional Airport over in Mt. Vernon. Mears Field is going to get crowded fast."

Evan called that information up to Mark.

Mark didn't swear much, but began cursing a blue streak on that one; Evan could practically hear him continue despite Mark having let go the transmit key. Moments later, Evan spotted the King Air diving down from its position toward the small airport along the Skagit River. Apparently they were on their own while Mark had a word or twenty with the fly-in's organizers.

The fire had burned fifteen thousand acres, not counting the five thousand currently on fire and headed right for them.

Darkness descended, though it was still a half hour to sunset. The sun wasn't strong enough to do more than color the overhanging pall of smoke and ash. Four of the helos not certified for night flying headed back to the airport.

The big fixed wing tankers were grounded as well. Running a high-speed jet two hundred feet above a wildfire on this terrain—in the dark—was a trick that made Evan glad he'd always been a ground-pounder.

"One hour of sleep. That's all I ask for," Evan muttered as he scraped more organics off the fireline, away from the fast approaching flames.

"Wimp!" Krista aimed a white-toothed smile from her smoke blackened face. "You had six hours sleep just two nights ago."

"I did, but my body doesn't seem to remember it for some reason."

"I remember a shower," she teased him.

"No you don't, Krista. You were out on your feet. I soaped and scrubbed your body and didn't even earn a happy moan for my troubles."

She slammed her Pulaski into the soil beside where his had stuck and together they managed to break free a thick clump of roots and toss it toward the far side of the firebreak. As they did so, she let out a deep throaty moan that galvanized his body despite his exhaustion.

She laughed at him as his libido raged him into breathlessness.

Krista was still moving faster and working harder than anyone else on the line, but she'd eased back from scary to merely impossible to keep up with.

"You doing better, Mama Krista?" he asked the next time they rested for a moment to chow down on a couple fistfuls of trail mix that Krista had stashed away somewhere. The chocolate chips had melted, making them a sticky mess that picked up the flavor of the soot on his palm, but he was past caring.

# # #

"I am," Krista blinked in surprise. She was doing better and it was suddenly disorienting.

The fire had consumed her. She had no love for the town, no real connection to it anymore—nor had she for years.

"Now it's…just a fire?" Well mostly. "I still want to kick its flaming ass, but it's no longer destroying my past. I guess that happened a long time ago."

Evan offered her another handful of her own trail mix as the tendrils of smoke swirled about them. All up and down the line, the smokies would be doing the same, taking on hurried calories in preparation for the imminent arrival of the fire when there wouldn't be time.

"I lost so much here. I still am losing it," she waved toward the flames eating up her childhood memories one by one. "But it seems less important now."

As she said it, she knew why.

This man beside her.

This man who had cleaned her up in the shower. Who had trusted that she would be safe on the fire. Who hadn't let her out of his sight for more than a few moments in the last thirty-six hours because he cared that much that she *remained* safe.

Well, she cared that much about him. And that alone made the present more important than the past.

She glanced toward the fire, they still had a few more moments before they had to get back to it.

Krista rested a hand on Evan's chest and looked at him. He needed—

No, he deserved to know the last piece of the story.

"I know how it must feel to have lost your sister."

His face clamped down hard. He had the decency not to protest, only shaking his head once in denial, but it was clearly costing him.

"My father was dead within weeks of my starting my first fire season. My only true friend, the only person to ever really believe in me. He didn't use a rifle, but he might as well have. He had cancer but never treated it because we couldn't afford it. Never tried, never admitted to it. I found the hospital tests buried in his papers when I cleaned out the house. He held it together until I was gone."

Evan's face had shifted. His hand slipped up to cover her own on his chest. "That's why you fought against the fire the way you did."

She nodded, now speechless at his perfect understanding of her.

"It was erasing all you had left of your father."

Krista buried her face against his shoulder. She'd thought it would be easier if she said it, told him why. But it hurt so damn much. All the pain she'd been hiding throughout the two days on the fire, maybe throughout the decade she'd been fighting fire, poured out of her all at once.

She never cried. Not when she had received news of his death, not at his graveside, not when she'd sold the house and shop.

Now, against the shoulder of a man she'd known only a few months, it poured out of her. Not in great wracking sobs, but in streaming, silent tears.

Evan still held her one hand tightly against his chest, and wrapped his other around her shoulders. Held her tight despite the mess she was.

The heat of the tears washed away so much of the pain, but they didn't fix who she was. Didn't change that someone who looked like her could never deserve a man like Evan.

She shouldn't care.

Sure she was crazy about him. Hoped he stayed deluded about her for a good while longer.

But she did care.

Wanting what you can't have, Krista. The curse of her life.

She'd wanted a good wife for Pop, but Mom had skipped mere months after Krista was born.

She'd wanted prosperity for him too, but that had never come.

She'd wanted to fit in, to belong, but by sixth grade she'd been the tallest girl in the school—including the high school— and twice as wide.

Firefighting with Mount Hood Aviation was the only place she'd ever fit in, doing a man's job with her man-strong body.

Firefighting…and curled up against Evan Greene in full gear, stinking of sweat and char.

Oh god. That freshened the font of tears she couldn't seem to stem. When she eventually lost Evan—when he woke up, saw who she really was and it finally ended—it was going to rip her completely apart.

"Krista, Babe?"

No one had ever called her "Babe." That's what you called pretty little things.

"Fire's coming. You up for it?"

She nodded against his shoulder, relishing his easy strength for just a moment longer.

Then she yanked herself free from his grasp and wiped at her face, glad that the darkness and, soon, a fresh layer of soot would hide their tracks.

"Let's do it," she managed on a hoarse croak that sounded like a dying frog. Real attractive.

He nodded in acknowledgment, then did one of those crazy Evan things.

Hooking a hand behind her neck, he kissed her so hard and deep that she had vertigo when he abruptly let go and turned for the fire with one of those cat-ate-the-canary grins of his.

It was only as he walked toward the leading edge of the fireline that her body reported where his other hand had been.

She dusted at her Nomex fire shirt to smear the sooty handprint he'd left over her breast.

Then she too turned toward the fire.

To stand beside her man for as long as he was willing to stand beside her.

# # #

By the time the sun rose and they'd been on the fire for forty-eight straight hours without a break, the smokies were done.

Evan felt as if he'd been shattered, from the inside out. Every movement hurt. His body ached. His hands and feet were blistered and bandaged.

Ox was limping. Ant-man's face was bloody from where a bad step had sent him tumbling down a slope—only a slash pile had stopped him from a far longer and more probably lethal fall. Akbar sat back against a boulder, head back, massaging a knee, and grinning like a goddamn idiot.

They all were.

The battle had raged back and forth across the ridges of Goat Mountain. Evan tried to estimate how many times he'd climbed it as he'd raced to beat the latest break in the line. Twenty-five hundred feet from valley floor to the peak, at least six times that he could remember, but it could have just as easily been ten. Another couple trips up and down and he'd have climbed the height of Everest.

Pass. He'd be lucky if he could walk another dozen steps.

He stood beside Krista, looking down. They had their arms around each other's waist and Evan would be content to stand like that for a long time.

Of all the smokies, they were the only ones not looking toward the still sparking and sizzling, but fully contained, fire.

Instead they stood alone on the south side of Goat Mountain's summit.

The others admired what they'd done—they'd beaten the monster. Again.

To the south, nearly five thousand feet below them, the narrow slice of the Skagit River valley wandered through the towering peaks of the North Cascades. The trees were dark green with mid-summer, but the river was bright beneath the high sun, only thinly softened by the last of the fire's smoke drifting lazily upward.

From this distance, they could see Concrete sitting inside a wide bend of the river.

"There's a joke about Concrete," Krista spoke softly beside him.

"Tell me."

"Most of the town is down in the Skagit's flood-plain. A lot of old single- and double-wide manufactured homes. We say one of the advantages of living there is that you never have to clean your house." Like a good storyteller, she left a pause for him to fill.

"Never?"

"Nope. You just wait for the Skagit to flood each spring. Then you open the front and back door and it washes the place clean."

He chuckled dutifully. "Small towns."

They watched the vintage planes climbing up out of the field. With the helos and air tankers no longer on site, they'd opened up the air space and everyone was making a circle out to see the results of the burn. This was a year of the fly-in that would be talked about for a long time.

He made a point of waving at each one as it passed overhead and waggled its wings at them.

"Let's go," he suggested.

"Where?"

He nodded down the slope.

"Into Concrete? On purpose?" she made her voice sound horrified.

"Henderson said we get a couple days off. I'd like to see where you grew up."

"Do I get to see where you grew up?"

He shrugged, surprised at how small a pinch remained. "Sure, as long as we don't have to meet my parents."

"Deal."

Evan wondered at how easily they were both moving beyond their past. Until now it had so defined his every action, but with Krista beside him he now understood that the past didn't matter. What mattered was who he'd become and who he'd be in the future.

He looked at Krista in surprise.

"What?"

He shook his head and simply let himself enjoy her stunning blue eyes.

Some things he wasn't ready to say, even if he was thinking them.

Chapter 15

*T*he *town of Concrete* went nuts. It was the only way Krista could describe it.

Once the helos had fished them and their gear off the top of the mountain—and they'd slept the clock around—several of the smokies decided a trip up the Skagit to the fly-in would be fun.

She suspected that Evan was behind all of the sudden interest, but she couldn't prove it.

It took a little bit of shifting gear and personnel at the airport. The helos and most of the smokies headed south, back to the MHA air base for their days off. But they convinced Doug and Terry to bring their black-and-flame painted DC-3, *Jump M1*, up to the fly-in for the second day of the event.

Once they were on the ground, she got clear of the plane as fast as she could. The seventy-year-old bird had created its own sensation, far and away the largest plane to come to the fly-in, which was fine.

Krista wanted no part of it.

But there were disadvantages to being so tall, broad, and blond. In addition to scaring off most men—though not Evan as he'd proven most satisfyingly once they woke up this morning—it also made her easy to pick out in any crowd.

Krista was recognized.

Mayor Veronica Tam now Nelson had been the head cheerleader for the Concrete Lions—thin, pretty, and popular. But seeing how she'd been letting herself be treated was the reason that Krista had ultimately epoxied the quarterback into his locker.

"Krista! I haven't seen you since…"

Pop's funeral. Veronica had been one of the few to attend other than herself. When Krista had finally thought to ask, Veronica's answer had surprised her.

"When you locked up Brian, I finally understood that I had some value. It took me a while, but I got rid of him and found myself a decent guy. I'm here for you, not your dad. I hope that's okay."

Still the only real friend Krista had ever made in Concrete. Odd to call one conversation ten years ago a friendship, but it was.

"What brings you home?" Veronica wanted to know.

"I was in the area," she'd evaded.

Then Evan, damn him, leaned in with that charming smile of his and whispered to Veronica. "Number Two smokejumper," then he pointed up to the scorched scalp of Goat Mountain looming high above the Skagit River valley.

Veronica's jaw dropped; her gaze swinging back and forth between the fire that had come within hours of forcing her entire town to evacuate and Krista's own face.

Krista was hard pressed not to blush.

"I forgot you were a smokejumper," Veronica whispered in shocked awe.

"Number Two on the top team flying," Evan gleefully put in.

Krista was on the verge of fisting his ribs, maybe hard enough to crack a couple, when he kissed her cheek.

"Best damn smokie I've ever jumped with."

Her surprise stopped her intent to perform mayhem upon him.

That's when the place went nuts.

Akbar had already gone south to spend his days off with Laura, so Krista was the senior member of the team. Everyone instantly assumed she'd been the lead smokie as well as Incident Commander of the entire firefight that had ultimately included a dozen aircraft and well over a hundred people.

Ox, Ant-man, Nick the Greek, and Evan were suddenly her personal entourage and weren't helping her efforts in the least about fixing the misunderstanding.

The pilots were over with their DC-3, talking pilot things with the other fliers—the immaculate seventy-year-old plane was a huge hit.

But for the "Lead Smokie" and her collection of men, suddenly nothing was good enough.

Tacqueria Los Jarritos, the best Mexican food in the Pacific Northwest, was serving up their killer burritos in smokie-sized portions. Pints of Boundary Bay stout appeared at their sides.

While they ate, the Concrete Lions High School Marching Band played along the airfield, occasionally having to scamper for cover as planes returned from flying over the extinguished fire.

"The Lions?" Evan raised his voice to ask over a slightly off-key but very cheery version of *Louie Louie*.

"The Concrete Lions. School mascot."

Then that crazy smile of his appeared.

"What?"

"Krista the Mama Lion!" he declared.

"No!"

"Yes!" Ox jumped in. "Rook! That's perfect!" And he and Evan high-fived.

"No!" she tried to protest once more to no avail, already knowing it was a lost cause. This piece of the past, this place, would now follow her for her entire jumping career. Though maybe that wasn't a completely bad thing. She did love these hills and the river. Maybe when she finally retired she'd build a cabin out here and spend some time learning the new forest.

Whatever else the fire had felt like, the countryside had felt like home—a place so familiar that she would always belong no matter how long the absence. Or how much of it was torched. The forest was always changing, and this was a natural one. What was unnatural was that they'd stopped it.

Once the marching band was done, the PA come on.

Krista turned to look at the announcing stand—the flatbed of a rusting lumber truck—when she recognized Veronica's voice. The Mayor thanked the marching band and then...

Mayor Veronica Nelson announced that the smokies who'd killed the Bell Creek Fire and saved the town were on site.

Krista was going to kill her one high school friend.

The crowd roared with approval. In moments everyone was on their feet all around the airfield, cheering and clapping.

Veronica was waving her up to the platform.

No goddamn way! She shook her head hard and kept her seat.

She was on her feet before she realized that Ox and Evan were lifting her up.

"They love you," Ox told her.

"No they don't." Krista knew from long experience that she was not beloved of the people of Concrete. She'd never fit in anywhere other than as an MHA smokie.

"Their loss," Evan said as he began using that Special Forces' strength to walk her toward the stand.

She tried to bolt, but Ox, Ant-man, and Nick were right there behind her. Still, she might have tried to fight them, but Evan's arm wrapped possessively around her waist was confusing her.

"What do you mean their loss?" she managed as her fellow smokies—who she swore to hate forever more—continued nudging her toward the platform.

"Should be obvious, Mama Lion."

Krista shook her head.

It wasn't.

The ongoing cheers and applause were turning into a blur around her.

Somewhere a chant had started as more locals recognized her and it was gaining speed, "Krista! Krista!" No one had ever done that before.

They reached the base of the little ladder that had been propped up as a set of stairs onto the lumber truck's flatbed.

Evan pulled her around to face him as the chants and applause continued.

"It's their loss, Krista, if they don't love you. Because I do and it's about the best feeling of my life."

"*About* the best feeling?" He loved her? Was he just saying it or—

"I expect when we get married it will feel even better."

All she could do was blink. Then she managed a gasp. "But...you haven't asked!" Did she even want him to? She knew the answer to that.

And realized that the question didn't matter worth a damn.

All that mattered was the answer.

"Yes!" she shouted and dragged him into a kiss.

The crowd erupted with cheers.

Beneath the roar she pulled back to look into those dark eyes and knew that Evan Greene would take the future just as seriously as he'd taken both of their pasts.

"That's a commitment, Lover."

"Damn straight, Mama Lion."

Krista kissed him quickly and climbed the ladder, waving the other smokies to climb up behind her.

"Lee the Ant-man."

"Nick the Greek."

"Gustav the Ox," she introduced each one as they reached the platform and the crowd roared and cheered.

Then she looked deep into Evan's eyes as he stepped up beside her and Krista knew.

This is what forever felt like.

This is what it felt like to leave behind the out-sized girl and embrace the powerful woman.

"And this…" she waited for the crowd to still. "This is Lover Boy."

"Lover Boy?" Ox asked in surprise. "Yes!" He crashed a fist into Evan's shoulder.

Evan groaned as the crowd laughed and cheered.

But his smile was all for her.

And best of all, she'd be reminded of that every single time his new name echoed down the fireline.

About the Author

M. L. Buchman has over 50 novels and 30 short stories in print. His military romantic suspense books have been named Barnes & Noble and NPR "Top 5 of the year" and twice Booklist "Top 10 of the Year," placing two titles on their "Top 101 Romances of the Last 10 Years" list. He has been nominated for the Reviewer's Choice Award for "Top 10 Romantic Suspense of the Year" by RT Book Reviews and was a 2016 RWA RITA finalist. In addition to romance, he also writes thrillers, fantasy, and science fiction.

In among his career as a corporate project manager he has: rebuilt and single-handed a fifty-foot sailboat, both flown and jumped out of airplanes, and designed and built two houses. Somewhere along the way he also bicycled solo around the world.

He is now making his living as a full-time writer on the Oregon Coast with his beloved wife. He is constantly amazed at what you can do with a degree in Geophysics. You may keep up with his writing by subscribing to his newsletter at www. mlbuchman.com.

Daniel's Christmas *(excerpt)*

Daniel Drake Darlington III pushed back further into the armchair and hung on for dear life. Without warning the seat did its best to eject him forcibly onto the floor. Only the heavy seatbelt, that was threatening to cut him in half he'd pulled it so tight, kept him in place.

"You never were the best flier."

Daniel glared at President Peter Matthews as Marine One jolted sharply left. They occupied the two facing armchairs in the narrow cargo bay of the VH-1N White Hawk helicopter. The small, three-person couch along the side was empty. The two Marine Corps crew chiefs and the two pilots sat in their seats at the front of the craft.

"I'm fine," Daniel managed through gritted teeth. "I just don't like helicopters."

President Peter Matthews sat back casually. Apparently all the turbulence that the early winter storm could hand out had not interfered with his boss' enjoyment of Daniel's discomfiture.

"And why would that be?"

The President knew damn well why his Chief of Staff hated these god-forsaken machines. Even if Marine One was probably the single safest and best maintained helicopter on the planet, he hated it from the depths of his soul along with all of its brethren of the rotorcraft category.

"My very first flight. I suffered—" a jaw rattling shake, "a bad concussion. Then we crashed."

"Yes," the President stared contemplatively at the ceiling less than foot over their heads.

Daniel kept his head ducked down so that he didn't bang it there as they flew through the next pocket of winter turbulence.

"That was one of Emily's finer flights."

And it had been. If the helicopter had been flown by anyone of lesser skill than Major Emily Beale of the Special Operations Aviation Regiment, Daniel knew he'd have been dead rather than merely bruised and battered. Thankfully the Army trained the pilots of the 160th SOAR exceptionally well, even better than the four Marines flying the President's personal craft. And Major Beale was the best among them, except for perhaps her husband.

The tape of that flight and the much more fateful flight a bare two weeks later had become mandatory training in the Army's Special Operations helicopter regiment. To this day he knew his life would have ended if he'd been aboard for that second fiery crash. The crash that had taken the First Lady's life a year ago.

But that didn't make him like this machine one whit better.

"There's home." President Matthews nodded out the window just like any tourist. Any tourist who was allowed to fly over the intensely restricted airspace surrounding the White House.

Daniel managed to look toward the window as the helicopter banked sharply to the left. Please, just let them land safely and get out of this storm. The White House did look terribly cheery. November 30th, she wasn't sporting her Christmas décor yet, but she was a majestic building, brilliantly lit, perched in the middle of the most heavily guarded park on the planet. Another jolt and he squeezed his eyes shut.

He did manage to force his eyes open as they settled flawlessly onto the lawn with barely the slightest rocking on the shock absorbers.

In moments the door slid open and a pair of Marines stood at sharp attention in their dress uniforms as if the last day of November were a sunny summer day, and not blowing freezing rain at eleven o'clock at night.

Daniel stumbled out and managed to resist the urge to kneel and kiss the ground. For one thing, it would stain the knees of his suit. For another, the President would laugh at him. Okay, he'd laugh even more than he already was.

Both feet on the ground, Daniel found himself. Managed to pull on his Chief-of-Staff cloak so to speak. He grabbed his briefcase and kept his place beside the President as they headed toward the South Entrance. They each carried umbrellas of only marginal usefulness that the Marines had thoughtfully provided. Now that they were on the ground, Daniel didn't mind the cold rain in his face. It meant he was alive.

"I'd suggest turning in right away, sir. We have an early start tomorrow."

The President clapped him on the shoulder, "Yes, Mom."

"Your mother is over in Georgetown."

"Well, I'm not going to call you 'dear' so don't get your hopes up there."

Daniel had come to really like the President. Even at the end of a brutally long day, including a flight to Kansas City, then Chicago, and back, he remained upbeat with that inde-fatigable energy of his. He was easy to like. There'd now be no oil workers' strike in Kansas City and his Chicago dinner speech had benefited the new governor immensely.

"You go to bed too, Daniel."

"Just going to drop off this paperwork," he held up his briefcase.

The President headed for the Grand Staircase and Daniel turned down the white marble hall and headed over to the West Wing.

Somewhere behind them in the dark, the helicopter roared back to life and lifted into the night.

# # #

The phone hammered him awake. Daniel came to in his office chair with the phone already to his ear.

Someone was speaking rapidly. He caught perhaps one word in three. "CIA. Immediate briefing. North Korea."

He must have made some intelligible reply as moments later he was listening to a dial tone.

Daniel rubbed at his eyes, but the vista didn't change. Large cherry wood desk. Mounds of work in neatly stacked folders that he'd sat down to tackle after the long flight. His briefcase still unopened on the floor beside him. Definitely the Chief of Staff's office. His office. Nightmare or reality? Both. Definitely.

Phone. He'd been on the phone.

The words came back and, now fully awake, Daniel started swearing even as he grabbed the handset and began dialing.

Maybe he could blame all this on Emily Beale. In the three short weeks she'd been at the White House, Daniel had risen from being the First Lady's secretary to the White House Chief of Staff and it was partly Emily's fault. As if his life had been battered by a tornado. Still felt that way a year later.

Okay, call it mostly her fault.

As he listened to the phone ringing in his ear, it felt better to have someone to blame. He rubbed at his eyes. A year later and he still didn't know whether to curse Major Beale or thank her.

Maybe he could make it all her fault.

"Yagumph."

"Good morning, Mr. President."

"Is it morning?" The deep voice would have been incomprehensibly groggy without the familiarity of long practice.

Daniel checked his watch, barely morning. "Yes, sir!" he offered his most chipper voice.

"Crap! What? All of 12:03?"

"12:10, sir." They'd been on the ground just over an hour.

"Double crap!" The President was slowly gaining in clarity, maybe one in ten linguists would be able to understand him now.

"Seven more minutes of sleep than you guessed, sir."

"Daniel?"

"Yes, Mr. President?"

"Next time Major Beale comes to town, I'm sending you up on one of her training rides."

"Sounds like fun, sir." If he had a death wish. "Crashing in the Lincoln Memorial Reflecting Pool is definitely an experience I can't wait to relive." The Major was also the childhood friend of the President, so he had to walk with a little care, but not much. The two of them were that close.

"Time to get up, sir, the CIA is coming calling. They'll be here in twenty minutes."

"I'll be there in ten." A low groan sounded over the phone. "Make that fifteen." The handset rattled loudly as he missed the cradle. Daniel got the phone clear of his ear before the President's handset dropped on the floor.

Daniel hung up and considered sleeping for the another fifteen minutes. There was a nice sofa along the far wall sitting in a close group with a couple of armchairs, but he'd have to stand up to reach it. All in strong, dusky red leather, his secretary's doing after discovering Daniel had no taste. Janet had also ordered in a beautiful oriental rug and several large framed photographs. Even on the first day she'd known him well enough to chose images of wide-open spaces. He missed his family farm, but the photos helped him when D.C. was squeezing in too hard.

If he didn't stand and resisted the urge to seek more sleep, all that remained was to consider his desk. Its elegant cherry wood surface lost beneath a sea of reports and files.

Fifteen minutes. He could read the briefing paper on Chinese coal, review tomorrow's agenda which, if he were lucky, might stay on schedule for at least the first quarter hour of a planned fourteen-hour day. Or he could just order up a giant burn bag and be done with the whole mess.

He picked up whatever was on top of the nearest stack.

An Advent calendar.

Janet, had to be.

Well, the woman had taste. It was beautiful; encased in a soft, tooled-leather portfolio and tied closed with a narrow red ribbon done up in a neat bow. He pulled a loose end and opened the calendar. Inside were three spreads of stunning hand-painted pictures on deep-set pages. He took a moment to admire the first one.

It was a depiction of Santa and his reindeer. Except Santa might have been a particularly pudgy hamster and the reindeer might have been mice with improbable antlers. One might have had a red nose, or he might have had his eggnog spiked; the artist had left that open to interpretation. A couple of rabbits were helping to load the sleigh. Little numbered doors were set in the side of the sleigh, as well as in a nearby tree, and in the snow at the micedeer's paws. The page was thick enough that a small treat could be hidden behind each little door.

He shook the calendar lightly and heard things rattling. Probably little sweets and tidbits to hit his notorious sweet tooth.

The day Janet retired he'd be in so much trouble. Not only did she manage to keep his life organized, she also managed to make him smile, even when things were coming apart at the seams. Midnight calls from the CIA for immediate meetings didn't bode well, yet here he was dangerously close to enjoying the moment.

He started to open the little door with a tiny golden number "1" on the green ribbon pull tab. The door depicted a candy-cane colored present perched high on the sleigh.

"Don't do that."

He looked up.

A woman stood in the doorway, closely escorted by one of the service Marines. A short wave of russet hair curled partly over her face and trickled down just far enough to emphasize the line of her neck. Her bangs ruffled in a gentle wave covering one eye. The eye in the clear shone a striking hazel against pale skin. She wore a thick, woolen cardigan, a bit darker than her hair, open at the front over an electric blue turtleneck that appeared to say, "Joy to the World." At least based on the letters he could see.

"Don't do what?"

"Don't open it early," she nodded toward the calendar in his hands. "That's cheating."

He double-checked his watch. "It's twelve-eighteen on December first. That's not cheating."

"Not until nighttime, after sunset. That's what Mama always said."

"And your Mama is always right?"

"Damn straight." Though her expression momentarily belied her cheerful insistence.

He glanced at the Marine. "Kenneth. Does she have a purpose here?"

She sauntered into his office as if it were her own living room and an armed Marine was not following two paces behind her. More guts than most, or a complete unawareness of how close she was to being wrestled to the ground by a member of the U.S. Military.

"Remember what they say about the book and the cover?"

"Sure, don't judge." He inspected her wrinkled black corduroys and did his best not to appreciate the nice line they made of her legs.

She dropped into one of the leather chairs in front of his desk and propped a pair of alarmingly green sneakers with red laces on the cherry wood. At least they were clean. All she'd need to complete the image would be to pop a bright pink gum bubble at him. And maybe some of those foam slip-on reindeer antlers. He offered her a smile as she slouched lower in the chair. In turn, she offered him a clear view most of the way to her tonsils with a massive yawn.

She managed to cover it before it was completely done.

"Sorry, I've been up for three days researching this. Director Smith said I should bring it right over." She waved a slim portfolio at him that he hadn't previously noticed.

CIA Director Smith. Well, that explained who she was. Whatever lay in that portfolio was the reason he'd only had forty-five minutes of sleep so far tonight. And he'd spent that slumped in his chair. He did his best to surreptitiously straighten his jacket and tie.

"You've been researching." Maybe a prompt would get her to the point more quickly.

"Yes, Mr. Darlington. I'm Dr. Alice Thompson, with dual masters in Afghani and Mathematics at Columbia. Which makes me a dueling master. PhD in digital imaging at NYU and an analyst for the CIA. Which means something, but I have no idea what. The reason you're awake right now is to meet with me."

"No, the reason I'm awake right now is to meet with both you and the President."

"The President?" She jerked upright in her chair, her feet dropping to the floor. "No one said anything about that to me." She twisted right and left as if seeking a place to hide.

"And it's Dr. Darlington of Tennessee. Degrees in agriculture at University of Kentucky—"

"Go Wildcats," she mumbled automatically without losing her somewhat frantic expression.

Daniel wondered how a New York girl living in D.C. would know that, but didn't sidetrack to ask.

"Poli Sci at Yale, and socio-economics at Princeton where I had the great opportunity to study cooperative economic game theory with Dr. Nash." And why he felt the need to brag to this lady once again settling in his office chair like she was hanging out in a college dorm room remained a bit of a mystery. He didn't feel sleepy anymore watching her across the mess that he called a desk. Instead he found himself truly smiling.

"You didn't really wake the President for this meeting, did you?" Her voice was little more than a whisper as she struggled to fight her body upright in the chair. She leaned forward far enough for the cardigan to fall open and reveal that the front of her turtleneck actually read "Oy to the World."

Daniel offered her his blandest smile and would have admired how snugly the material clung to her frame, but he couldn't look away from those hazel-green eyes.

"You did wake him?" her whisper more than a little panicked.

"I wish he hadn't." The President entered as she spoke. "Does this mean I can I go back to bed?"

For more information on this and other titles,
please visit www.mlbuchman.com

Other titles by this author

20179348R00115

Printed in Poland
by Amazon Fulfillment
Poland Sp. z o.o., Wrocław